J. NATHAN

Edited by Stephanie Elliot
Proofed by Gem's Precise Proofreads

Cover Design by Kate Farlow at Y'all. That Graphic.
Cover Photo by Brian Kaminski
Cover Model Jake Hobbs

First Edition October 2020

For my son, the funniest person I know. There is no one in this world I would rather spend my time with than you.

PROLOGUE

Kresley

I lay on my bed, the soft sounds of Paris trickling in from my open window. And though Andre wouldn't approve of an open window—after he'd already secured the premises for the night—sometimes a girl just needed to let Paris in.

I contemplated pulling up another movie to stream, but I had an early class in the morning so I pulled my long blonde hair into a messy knot, crawled under my comforter, and set the alarm on my phone. I closed my eyes, thinking about my presentation the following day. I hated speaking in front of a class, but it was a necessary evil to graduate.

Just as I was about to doze off, I heard a loud thud in the sitting room and someone yelled, "Down on the ground!"

I jerked up.

"Where is she?" a deep French voice ordered.

More muffled sounds.

Then…

Bang!

I jumped at the sound of a gunshot as a shiver tore up my spine. I looked around my room frantically, knowing it was a matter of seconds before my closed door swung open. I slipped out of bed, snatching the knife off the dish with the apple core beside my bed.

With shaking hands, I crawled underneath the bed and onto the cold hardwood floor. My body shook as I lay in a ball trying to make myself as small as I could. My comforter didn't reach the floor, so all someone needed to do was bend down and they'd see me.

Fuck.

Footsteps moved in the sitting room, nearing my closed bedroom door.

Please be Andre. Please be Andre.

My bedroom door squeaked open and heavy footsteps moved across my floor. I lay still, but my pulse thrashed throughout my body, and my labored breathing threatened to give me away.

An eerie silence descended over my room. Was it Andre? If so, why wasn't he speaking?

A hand grabbed my ankle.

I screamed, my legs kicking wildly as I tried to free myself. But another hand grabbed my other ankle and I was dragged out from under the bed. I tucked the knife behind my back, gripping it tightly as my legs flailed in an attempt to break loose. But he was too strong, holding my ankles like two impenetrable vice grips. I gave up the fight and lay on my floor with my chest rising and falling as I stared up at a man dressed in black with a black mask covering all but his eyes. Another man dressed the same stood in the doorway.

"Where's Andre?" I asked, my voice cracking and sounding nothing like my own.

They scoffed under their masks, exchanging a knowing glance.

Bile shot up the back of my throat, knowing with every fiber of my being that the gunshot had been for Andre. Tears glazed my eyes. "What do you want?"

"What do you think we want?" the man at my feet

asked, his French accent taunting me with the very thing I adored about France.

"I can get you whatever you want," I assured him, fighting to keep my voice from cracking.

He released my ankles but quickly grabbed my hand that didn't hold the knife and yanked me to my feet. I kept the knife held against my back, terrified he'd see it. He didn't, pushing me to the nearest wall and slamming my back to it.

My body trembled.

Andre wasn't coming to save me.

No one was coming to save me.

My only saving grace was the knife in my hand. But did I have the nerve to use it with his partner in the door ready to hurt me if I did?

The man pressed his chest to mine, pushing me harder into the wall as he leaned into my ear. His sweaty putrid scent strangled me, and I fought not to gag. "Tsk, tsk, tsk." His spit brushed my ear. "*Le fou de fortune*," he whispered. *Fortune's fool.* "I want you to have your parents wire ten million dollars into an off-shore account."

"I can do that," I assured him as I tightened my grip on the knife behind my back.

"I wasn't asking."

I closed my eyes, willing back the tears that fell regardless.

"Then..." His hand slipped between my thighs, cupping me. "I want to know what a rich American college girl feels like."

I swallowed hard.

This wasn't happening. This was a sick dream I'd soon wake up from.

Bang!

The sound of another gunshot tore through my apartment.

My eyes snapped open as I jumped, despite the weight pressed against me.

"What the fuck?" the man holding me said as he turned to look to his partner in the doorway.

I yanked the knife from behind my back and stabbed at him, not even sure where I was hitting since his hands flew up to protect his masked-covered face.

He reeled back with a roar, his hands cupping his mask with blood staining his fingers.

Now that I was no longer pinned to the wall, my eyes shot around, desperate for a way out. His partner blocked the doorway holding his chest as a pool of blood spread beneath his hand. I jumped over my bed toward the open window. I was on the second floor but I'd jump. It was my only option.

Just then, a barrage of footsteps in the distance manifested and shouting in French warned that the police were coming.

The man I'd stabbed rushed to his partner. He held his face with one hand and grabbed his partner under the arm with the other. He turned to me. "This isn't over, *le fou de fortune.*"

And just like that, they disappeared out my bedroom door.

After the initial shock wore off, I scrambled unsteadily to the door to check that they were indeed gone. My apartment was empty but the front door was wide open. Andre sat on the floor with his back against the wall and blood soaking through the front of his white shirt. His eyes were barely open and his gun lay in his lap.

"Andre!" I screamed, dropping the bloody knife to the floor with a clatter as I rushed over to him.

Four police officers burst through the open front door.

"We need an ambulance!" I yelled.

"Who did this?" one of them asked.

"They just ran out!" Tears poured from my eyes, relieved the cavalry had arrived but so shaken up I could no longer hold it together.

The officers spread out, two searching around my apartment while the others disappeared back into the hallway.

I wrapped my arms around Andre. He'd been like a father to me for the past two and a half years while I'd been studying abroad—not to mention the years prior as my security as a kid. But not until tonight had he ever taken a bullet for me. "You're gonna be okay," I assured him, having absolutely no idea if that was the truth.

"I know, Kresley," he whispered. "I'm so sorry I couldn't stop them."

"You saved me," I assured him, gently cupping his paling cheek. "They would have gotten me if you didn't shoot that man."

"I was caught off guard. They avoided the cameras. When they burst through the door, I wasn't armed."

"*Shhh*, Andre." I ran my hand over his gray hair. "It's okay. I'm okay."

But I wasn't okay. I was far from it. But all that mattered in that moment was that Andre lived.

I was no one.

He couldn't die protecting no one.

CHAPTER ONE
Six Months Later
Kresley

I stood in the center of my new dorm room at Remington University in my home state of California. My eyes took in the cinderblock walls, small desk, and bare mattress.

"Well, at least they gave you a single," my mother offered, taking in the small size of the room.

I swear I wasn't a snob, but this room was smaller than my walk-in closet at home. "There's that."

"You know this is the only way to ensure your safety. Getting you that apartment was a huge mistake. If you'd been immersed with the other students, they wouldn't have been able to…" Her voice drifted off. I wasn't the only one who hated to think about what happened in France.

"It's no one's fault, Mom," I said, not wanting to discuss the nightmare I'd lived through.

She sighed. "I just wish you'd stay at home, that's all. I finally had you back and now you're leaving again. I can't keep you safe if you're here."

I dropped down onto the bare mattress as rap music from a nearby room echoed in the hallway. "I need to do this."

She understood. She knew I needed to keep going in order to move on. I wouldn't let those men win. I couldn't. "At least Santa Barbara is a beautiful place."

"I'd still feel a lot better if Andre was with me," I said.

She tipped her head. "Honey, you know the deal. You're only here if you have more precautions in place. Andre was getting too old to protect you."

She was right. He *was* getting old. And slow. And distracted. But I needed him for more than just protection. He had been the closest person to me while I explored an unfamiliar country on my own for the first time in my life. He'd been there the first time I'd visited the Eiffel Tower and The Louvre. The first time a French guy tried to kiss me and take me back to his place. The first time a pickpocket tried to snatch my money. I owed Andre more than just my life.

"Your protection will be discreet, but always around—and *armed*," my mother said, adding the last part to drive home the point that Andre had been *un*armed when the men broke into my apartment. His gun was nearby, just not on him. A no-no in the field of security. And since the men had not been caught yet, I guess I appreciated the reassurance that my new security would be armed at all times. "Duffy and Stone have their orders," my mother continued. "They know where to be and when to be there. You will never be without someone."

"When do I get to meet them?"

She glanced around as if they were somehow hiding in my box of a room. "I'm sure they're around here somewhere. They've already been here for a few days preparing for your arrival."

I rolled my eyes, knowing it was for my own safety but hating that people needed to treat me like this precious gem when I wasn't. My *father* was rich. Billionaire rich. Which meant people wanted to kidnap me, his only daughter, and hold me for ransom. It came with the territory. It happened to professional athletes, actors, and rich businessmen all over the world more frequently than the general public ever knew. But I'd known the risk my whole life. It's why security accompanied me wherever I went. Yup, prom was real fun.

"Mrs. Hastings?"

My mom and I turned to the sound of a deep voice coming from my now open door.

A huge guy with a thick reddish goatee and shoulder-length slicked-back hair stood in the doorway. His tight black Henley and black cargo pants told me he wasn't just some floor mate coming to introduce himself. "Everything's set in place."

I looked to my mom. "What's everything?"

"Surveillance, ma'am," he answered for her.

"Kresley," I corrected him. "Not ma'am. I'm twenty-one, not eighty." I tried not to sound like a bitch, but I hated not knowing what was going on when it came to me. And the fact that I was only meeting this guy today, when I knew for a fact that my parents had interviewed both him and his partner weeks ago, pissed me off.

"Honey, this is Marco Duffy," my mother said.

"Should I call you sir, or is Marco okay?" I asked him.

"Marco's fine, ma'am."

"Dammit, Marco. Having a bodyguard is bad enough. Calling me ma'am is gonna piss me the hell off."

His lips twitched. "Noted, ma'am."

I growled low in my throat, unsure if I *was* pissed or amused.

"Well, now that introductions are out of the way," my mother interrupted, "we need to get your things brought up from the car."

"I've got Marco. I'm sure he wouldn't mind putting those big muscles to use since he's gonna be following me down there anyway," I assured her before glancing to Marco for confirmation.

"Not at all, ma'am."

I ignored his use of *ma'am*, having a feeling I'd sound like a broken record if I kept at it.

He followed me out of my room, weaving around students carrying their own boxes and luggage as we made our way to the stairwell at the end of the hallway.

"How old are you, Marco?"

"Thirty-five," he said as we took the stairs to the first floor.

"You married?"

"Yes," he said, opening the side door and checking the surrounding area before allowing me to proceed.

"Have any kids?" I asked.

"My wife's pregnant."

"Congratulations," I said as I followed him outside.

"Thank you," he said, though his eyes remained on our surroundings and not me.

"Did you go to college?" I asked as we stepped up to my mom's Mercedes SUV parked at the curb. I hit the key to unlock the doors and open the back door.

"No, ma'am. Military. Special Forces."

"Thank you for your service, Marco," I said. "Sorry you're stuck in college anyway. I'll try not to make it too boring for you."

"Boring's good," he assured me as he moved to the back of the SUV. "It means you're safe."

I didn't say anything as he reached in the back and pulled out several bins. I grabbed clothes on hangers and carried those over my shoulder as we made our way back upstairs.

It took a few hours, and multiple trips to retrieve all my belongings from the car, to unpack my things. When I finally said goodbye to my mother, she hugged me like she'd never see me again. I understood her trepidation in leaving me. I'd been home for six months where I didn't leave her sight—except for my counseling sessions. The last time we said goodbye, I'd been leaving for France—where I'd nearly been raped and kidnapped, and my bodyguard was shot. I let her hold me for as long as she needed. Truth be told, I needed it too.

Marco stayed outside as I decorated my walls with posters of beautiful white sand beaches and private islands. I placed framed photos on my desk. A couple of my parents and me on beaches in Greece, and a couple of us sailing along the Mediterranean. Those reminded me of happy times, and I hoped the images would bring me solace and give me a place to escape to if I felt the outside world suffocating me.

I switched on some country music, allowing Luke Bryan to drown out the rap music still playing down the hall as I climbed onto my desk chair and hung strands of tiny white lights around the perimeter of my room. Complete darkness at night wouldn't work for me. I needed some kind of light if there was any chance that I'd sleep. I pressed a tack into the corner of the room where the wall met the ceiling. I leaned in closer, my eyes narrowing on a small wire extending from the ceiling. I tugged on it.

My door flew open and Marco burst in. "What are you doing!?"

The air punched out of my lungs, startled by the unexpected intrusion. "Jesus Christ, Marco! Don't you knock?"

"Sorry, ma'am, I just—"

"Is this a camera?"

He shifted his weight from one foot to the other. "Yes."

"Are you watching me?"

"No."

I stepped down from the chair and stood on the floor, tipping my head back so I could look him into the eyes. I wasn't short. But he was massive. "Then how did you know to come in here?"

"An alert goes off if anyone touches the camera," he explained.

"How do I know you won't be watching me when I get undressed?"

"I wouldn't do that."

"How about if I bring a guy back here?"

He shook his head. "I'll search him before he comes in, but I won't watch the camera feed."

Though I understood the newest precaution, I'd never had a camera *in* my room. I hated the idea of losing my last shred of privacy. "Where are the other cameras?"

"In the hallway. By the front and rear entrances. In the front and rear stairwells. And, in the basement. If anyone gets in here, we'll know about it."

I couldn't be sure if I was relieved by the information or completely overwhelmed by it. "Did the school allow you to install cameras?"

"I don't care if they allow it, ma'am. Your safety's my only priority."

There was something reassuring about his blatant disregard for school rules and his determination to protect me. But, at the same time, it meant there was a reason to be so cautious. A reason to be overly prepared. A reason to fear for my safety—especially until the

French men were caught. "When do I meet your partner? You're clearly not on duty twenty-four hours a day."

"He's around."

"Where will you both be when you're not with me?" I asked.

His lips twisted as if he didn't want to say.

My eyes shot around my small room. "Well, I know you're not staying in here with me."

"We have our own rooms," he admitted. "I'm next door. He's across the hall."

"What about your wife? When will you see her?"

"She understands this is my job. And I assure you, when I'm on duty, you've got all of my attention."

"Do you really think they're going to track me here?"

"We have no idea if they were working alone or with other people. Do you have any idea how many kidnapping attempts happen every day, especially with powerful families?"

"Yes. That's why I've had security all my life."

He nodded, realizing I did understand. "Will you be staying in tonight?"

"It's not like I know anyone but you. So, yeah. I'm probably staying in."

"Can I have your phone?" he asked.

I walked over to my desk and grabbed it. "You're not already tracking it?"

"Yeah, we're tracking it. But I need you to have our numbers."

I unlocked my phone and handed it to him.

He punched the numbers into it. "Text or call me or Stone whenever you need to leave the room and one of us will accompany you."

"The bathroom is two doors down. I'm capable of braving the walk alone."

"*Whenever* you leave your room," he ordered.

"You're gonna get sick of my weak bladder."

"I can handle it."

I spent the rest of the evening organizing my clothes by colors since I had nothing better to do. At eight o'clock, there was a knock on my door. My eyes drifted to the camera in the corner of the room. Was I supposed to answer the door? Was I supposed to wait for Marco? I stalled, slowly moving to the door, assuming Marco would come out and check whoever was out there. But when I didn't hear anything, I spoke. "Who is it?"

"Elodie," a girl said. "Your RA."

I opened the door to find a skinny girl with fair skin, dark hair, and glasses smiling at me. "You must be Kresley."

"Hi." My eyes moved behind her, half expecting Marco to be standing there, but I was only met with more rap music blaring down the hall and other students passing by as they moved into their rooms.

"Welcome to Remington," Elodie said, pulling my attention back to her. "I hear you're a transfer. Where'd you transfer from?"

"I'm from California but I transferred from Paris."

Her eyes expanded behind her glasses, making her brown eyes even bigger in the lenses. "Sounds like a dream," she said.

More like a nightmare. "Yeah. Well, I'll be graduating from Remington at the end of the school year," I said with a smile that likely didn't reach my eyes. I prayed she didn't ask any more questions. I'd been guarded since Paris. I wished I wasn't, but my counselor assured me it was normal—as long as I gradually opened myself back up to people.

"You're a senior?" Elodie asked.

I nodded.

"What's your major?"

"Hospitality. I'd like to be an event planner."

"Sounds cool," she said, her eyes looking over my shoulder into my room. "Wow. It looks more like a beach resort in there than a dorm room. *Nice job.*"

I twisted to look inside. My light blue comforter with complementary throw pillows gave it a warm feel and matched the water in my posters. "Thanks."

"Well, I just wanted to come say hi," she said, as I turned back to her. "I'm at the end of the hall in 202. If you need anything at any time of day or night, that's what I'm here for. But, I just met Marco. He said he's your security?"

I nodded, knowing she was probably looking for answers I wasn't ready to give. "Yeah, if we could keep that quiet, I'd be forever grateful."

She zipped her fingers across her lips.

I smiled. "It was nice to meet you."

"You too." She turned to go.

"Hey, Elodie?"

She stopped and twisted back to me.

"What does everyone do around here for fun?"

"Half the campus is Greek. So, frat parties."

"Do people ever go off campus to bars or clubs?"

"Oh, sure. Noise is a great one. My roommate Alice and I are actually heading there later tonight if you'd like to come."

I'd never been so happy for an invite in my entire life. I hadn't been able to sleep well since Paris, so I'd been worried about my first night in a new place. But, dancing and drinking would definitely tire me out and help me with that. "I'd love to."

"We'll come by and get you around ten-thirty."

"Thanks, Elodie. I don't know anyone here, so I really appreciate this."

"Sure thing. It'll be fun." She smiled before turning away.

Even though attending Remington hadn't been part of my original plan, maybe, just maybe, everything would turn out okay after all.

CHAPTER TWO
Kresley

I sat in the backseat of Marco's Escalade behind tinted *and* bulletproof windows. Elodie and her roommate Alice sat on either side of me. They were both kind enough not to ask why I had a driver, more pumped to know that neither of them had to be the designated driver. I wore skinny jeans and a strapless green shirt with a necklace of three twisted strands of diamonds—a gift from my father for my sixteenth birthday. I wasn't sure what kind of place it was, so I didn't want to get too dressed up. But Elodie and Alice wore similar outfits, which made me feel better.

Alice turned to me, her long strawberry blonde hair falling over her shoulders as she did. She was Daphne to Elodie's Velma. I wondered if anyone else had ever noticed their uncanny resemblance to the mystery solvers? "So, you were in school in Paris?" Alice asked.

"Yeah."

"Was it tough to leave such a gorgeous place?" Elodie asked.

"Not really. I missed home." It wasn't a complete lie. I did miss home. But it clearly wasn't the reason I needed to leave.

The bar must've been only a few miles off campus because, before long, Marco pulled into a large parking lot with a ton of cars. Once he cut the engine, he jumped out of the driver's seat and pulled open the back door.

"Why thank you, kind sir," Alice said, sliding out first and giving him a little curtsy as she did.

I slipped out next. "Thanks, Marco."

Elodie followed. "Thanks, big man."

We all headed into the bar. Marco followed, staying a few feet behind us.

The bar was loud and crowded, and I knew instantly that crowded places were a bitch to stake out. Inwardly, I cringed, knowing my last-minute plans likely had Marco scrambling.

I followed the girls to a table on the far side of the bar. A waitress approached us before we even sat, shouting over the music to get our order.

We made small talk as we waited for our drinks and watched the people on the dance floor moving to the music. Alice and Elodie were seniors too. They'd been best friends since elementary school and decided to go to Remington together. They had the uncanny ability to speak at the same time and say the exact same thing which I found hysterical. I wished I had a friend like that, but growing up and attending school with other wealthy kids left little room to forge lasting authentic relationships. It was a lot of one-upping which I despised. It was probably why I had very few friends.

Our drinks arrived, and, ironically, we toasted to new friends.

"Selfie time," Alice said, holding up her phone so she could get us all into a picture.

"I'm sorry." I winced. "I can't take photos."

They exchanged a look, likely questioning their decision to invite the new girl. Because, at this point, everything about me screamed run the other way and avoid.

"It's not that I *can't* be in a picture," I explained. "I just can't have it posted online."

Since I was supposed to be in school in New York—as far as anyone following me on social media was concerned, I needed to keep a low profile. Staying off social media was condition number one if I wanted to finish school at Remington. And, truthfully, it wasn't really a hardship since I didn't stay connected with too many people.

"Are you in the witness protection program or something?" Alice blurted, probably finally fed up with all the mystery surrounding me.

Elodie shot her daggers

"Something like that," I offered, completely understanding her curiosity. I too would've had questions if one of them had transferred from Paris accompanied by her own bodyguards and drivers, and couldn't have her photo posted online.

"So, if I promise not to post this anywhere, you can be in it?" she asked.

I nodded.

"Deal."

We all squeezed together and Alice snapped the selfie. And as much as I appreciated her assurance that she wouldn't post it, it was just a matter of time before I needed to tell them the truth—especially if I wanted to hang out with them again.

We ordered a couple more drinks before Elodie and Alice were dragging me out onto the dance floor. And since I wasn't a big drinker, the alcohol had gone straight to my head. As I moved to the music, I glanced around, spotting Marco in the corner of the room—sticking out like a sore thumb in his dark clothes and obvious aversion to the club music pumping through the room.

Regardless, his presence still made me feel safe.

The girls and I danced to three or four more songs. And even though I was getting hot and sweaty, I was having so much fun. Once another song ended, I yelled to Alice and Elodie, "I've gotta pee."

Elodie pointed in the direction of the bathrooms.

"Thanks!" I made my way through the crowded dance floor to the hallway in the back corner of the bar and stepped into the back of the long bathroom line. I twisted around, spotting Marco standing where he could still see me. My leg began to bounce as I impatiently waited. The line was so long and I *really* needed to pee.

The door to the men's room opened. *The hell with it.* I stepped out of the ladies' line and rushed to the men's room where there was no one waiting. I stopped short, unintentionally blocking the guy inside from leaving. He moved to the side at the same time I did. I laughed. We tried again, moving to the other side. I laughed again and my head tipped back. My gaze collided with the bluest eyes I'd ever seen. They were teal—the color of beautiful Caribbean waters. But their owner wasn't laughing. He didn't even look amused.

He grabbed my arms to keep me still and moved around me. "This is the men's room," he said, his deep gravelly voice sending an unexpected surge of electricity through me.

"I know," I said, spinning to face him while trying to ignore my reaction to him. "I need to pee."

"It's disgusting in there," he assured me as he ran his hands through his dirty blond hair.

My eyes moved over his dark shirt and jeans that told me he wasn't trying too hard to look good…he just did. "Do I look like a high maintenance kind of girl to you?" I teased, hoping to get some kind of smile from him.

"High maintenance?" he asked as his eyes raked over my body, trying to decide.

His look elicited a heated path across my skin and I released a silent breath, unnerved by my unexpected reaction to him. That hadn't happened to me since…well, ever. The guys I'd spent time with were sons of my father's clients. Not guys who made me feel…anything.

His eyes landed on my necklace, narrowing coldly. "Oh, you're definitely high maintenance," he said with a chill to his voice.

"I am?"

"Not to mention completely desperate."

My eyes widened, our conversation taking a complete one-eighty.

"If picking up guys in bars is your thing, try playing it a little subtler. Because the way you're gawking at me is really freaking me out."

I sucked in a sharp breath as any remaining electricity fizzled out completely. *What an asshole.*

He said nothing more, just turned away from me and headed back through the crowd.

My insides twisted, a knot forming in my stomach as I walked into the men's room, locking the door behind me. *Did that really just happen?*

I left the men's room a couple minutes later, still unable to believe the nerve of that guy. I'd only been in Paris for two and a half years, but was that what meeting guys in the US was like now?

I made my way back to the dance floor, joining Elodie and Alice who were still dancing in the center of the crowd. I immersed myself in the music, dancing until sweat dripped down my hairline. I would sleep tonight if it was the last thing I did.

Out of the corner of my eye, I caught sight of the guy from the men's room staring at me from the bar. He stood with his arms crossed and his eyes locked on mine. A pretty brunette leaned into him, speaking into his ear. He reacted to her words by nodding or shaking his head, but his eyes never left mine.

I'll show you high maintenance and desperate.

I turned my attention back to the dance floor, never again looking back at him. He may have had the prettiest eyes I'd ever seen, but I had no time for judgmental pricks.

The girls and I danced until the lights turned on at closing time. We headed to the exit, following the flow of sweaty bodies. I glanced over my shoulder and Marco followed us out. As we walked to the SUV, my eyes shifted left and right, always on guard.

Marco hit the button and the doors unlocked. He pulled open the back door, and the three of us shuffled into the backseat.

"That was so much fun," I said once we were safely in the car and back on the road.

Elodie and Alice both turned to face me, both just as sweaty and their hair just as disheveled as mine must've been.

"We're so glad you came," they said at the same time. We all broke into laughter.

"So, is this a good time to ask about…?" Alice lifted her chin toward Marco in the front seat.

"It's totally fine if you don't want to say anything," Elodie added, shooting Alice a look.

"No, it's okay," I assured her. "I just ran into some trouble at my last school. Some people tried to kidnap me."

Alice gasped.

"They shot my bodyguard and would've taken me if the police hadn't shown up when they did. They took off and still haven't been found."

"Oh my God," Elodie said.

"Still want to hang out with me?" I asked lightheartedly.

"That was not what I was expecting," Alice said.

"I was hoping you were some Hollywood actress in disguise or something," Elodie said.

I shook my head. "Nothing that exciting. Just some sick people wanting to use me to get money from my dad," I said.

Elodie's face showed concern. "Do you think you're still in danger?"

I shrugged. "I don't know. Having security here is just a precaution."

"Do you carry a gun?" Alice asked.

"God, no. I'd hurt myself. But don't worry. I took self-defense classes and know how to kick a guy in the balls."

They laughed, and their laughter dissolved the heaviness in the car that the subject created.

A country song began to play on the radio. "I love this song!" Alice declared.

"Turn it up!" Elodie called to Marco who begrudgingly complied.

And just like that, it was as if the conversation never happened. We sang along to the music all the way back to the dorm, much to Marco's dismay.

Once we were back inside and had said our goodnights, Marco checked my room. When he stepped back out into the hallway, I said, "Thanks, Marco. For everything."

He nodded, and I hoped, despite the work he had to put into getting things ready for my night out, he realized how much I needed to find friends. He walked to his room to the left of mine. "Close the door," he ordered before stepping into his room.

I closed and locked my door, leaning my back against it and exhaling. I'd tried so hard to let loose and forget everything that happened to me. I lived in the moment, like my counselor had encouraged me to do at our last session. And, I laughed—like really laughed—for the first time in a long time.

But now I was alone.

My first night alone since Paris.

And I hoped to God I was as strong as I thought I was.

* * *

"Le fou de fortune…This isn't over…"

I jolted up, my body drenched in sweat and my heart racing. My eyes jumped around my dorm room expecting to see the masked Frenchman looming over me. But, the soft glow of the tiny lights around my ceiling confirmed that no one was in my room. My eyes shot to my door. It was still closed and locked.

Despite the rational side of my brain telling me it was just a nightmare, I still listened for Marco's footsteps.

But I didn't hear his footsteps. All I heard was the distant sound of salsa music drifting up from the room beneath mine.

A giant breath whooshed out of me, knowing I was safe. Knowing it was only a nightmare. Knowing *I got this.*

I climbed out of bed and stripped out of my sweat-drenched clothes. I grabbed a new T-shirt and shorts and pulled them on. And though I climbed back into bed, I knew the disappointing truth. The Frenchman was in my head. And sleep wouldn't come.

CHAPTER THREE
Kresley

I joined Elodie and Alice for breakfast the next morning. I glanced over at Marco, standing against a nearby wall in the dining hall with his arms crossed. It was glaringly obvious that he wasn't going to be able to blend in on campus. Sure, older people took classes. But they didn't live in the dorms. Go to dining halls. Stand in the back of classrooms. People *would* start asking questions. Especially once classes began tomorrow.

"I think I'm just gonna stay in for the rest of the day," I told Marco, once we returned to the dorm.

He nodded and walked to his door. He peeked over to be sure I'd gone into my room. I hadn't. "Get in your room and close the door," he ordered.

"So bossy," I said as I stepped inside. I could've sworn I heard him chuckle as I closed my door.

I spent the day watching movies, texting my parents, and napping. It was so much easier to sleep with sunlight casting through my window. It gave me a false sense of security that my brain needed in order to allow me to sleep.

"She's staying in for the day," Marco said to someone in the hallway. "But have your phone handy in case she changes her mind. Or needs the bathroom."

I climbed off my bed and moved to the door, pressing my ear to it to hear who he was talking to.

"A shadow under the door is a dead giveaway that you're in there," a deep voice said.

I looked down at the shadow caused by my feet. *Ah hell.* I opened the door and my breath caught in my throat.

The guy from the bar was standing in the hallway with Marco.

"What are *you* doing here?" I asked.

He looked at me with those teal eyes but showed no sign of recognition from our run-in outside the men's room. "Excuse me?"

"We met last night."

His bottom lip jutted out like he had no idea what I was talking about.

Seriously? He was gonna pretend he didn't know me and hadn't insulted me? Well, if that's how he was gonna play it, so was I. "Now that you mention it…" My eyes moved over his black cargo pants and black T-shirt molded to his broad chest. "The guy I met last night was a lot better looking." I drank in his dirty blond hair which was more tousled than it had been at the bar, like he'd just woken up. "And, he was taller. And a lot more built."

"This is my partner, ma'am," Marco explained.

I glared at Marco. "Kresley."

Unaffected by my annoyance with his use of *ma'am*, he continued. "This is Tristan Stone. He'll be with you when I'm not. We take turns securing locations before you arrive." He looked to Tristan and leveled him with his eyes. "Like he did last night at the bar."

I turned my glare to Tristan. *Asshole.*

He stared back at me, unfazed and not about to apologize for being deceptive.

"We were just discussing the week ahead," Marco explained to me.

"Oh, great. I have a request." My eyes moved between them. Tristan was younger and less bulky than

Marco, but no less athletic—even though I tried to make him feel less than. "Could you maybe try to look more like college students? The dark clothes make you stand out and, frankly, I don't want to be known as 'the girl with the bodyguards'."

"You *are* the girl with the bodyguards," Tristan clipped.

I cocked my head. "It's a request."

"Requests don't have to be granted," he fired back.

I opened my mouth to respond—

"We'll do what we can," Marco interrupted, clearly the calmer of the two. "As long as our weapons are concealed, I don't see why we can't try to blend in a little more." He turned around and walked to his room without another word.

I expected Tristan to follow him, but he didn't.

Perfect. "Let's just get this out of the way now then," I said to Tristan as Marco's door closed. "I don't know what your problem is with me—"

He scoffed. *Scoffed.*

I trudged on, getting more pissed by the second. "You work for me. A little common courtesy is not too much to ask."

He rolled his eyes.

God dammit. "If I can't trust you to protect me if things go wrong, my parents can find someone else who can."

His eyes narrowed. "What the hell does that mean?"

"This whole not knowing me thing after you blatantly disrespected me last night. Maybe I didn't know who *you* were at the bar, but you knew who *I* was. So, what gives?"

"Girls like you are what gives."

My head shot back so fast I was surprised it didn't slam into the door behind me. "Excuse me?"

"You were almost taken in France."

"Thanks for the recap. But I know what happened."

He shook his head, his teeth clenched and jaw ticking. "You're careless."

I pointed to myself. "I'm careless? I've got two bodyguards for Christ's sake."

"You get one life to live. Think about how you want to live it."

"Wow. So, now you're a philosopher?"

"It's no secret there are people out there who still may want to get to you."

"Yes. And that's why *you're* here."

"So, why the bar? Was it absolutely necessary to go out last night?" he asked.

"What I do is none of your business."

"The hell it isn't. I had to be there an hour and a half early—with added security—securing the place, not to mention overseeing every fucker they let in there."

I hated that I was being reprimanded. I'd only wanted to make friends and find a way to sleep. But maybe he was right. Maybe I should've considered how it would affect them. Maybe I should've considered the work they needed to put in every time I went somewhere.

"I could have been someone trying to get to you," he continued. "But you were standing there all drunk gazing at me like you would've gone home with me if only I asked."

My mouth parted, too stunned by his words to respond.

"And then that ridiculous necklace you wore. It must be worth tens of thousands of dollars. Way to stay off people's radars."

"I've been through enough counseling to know what happened to me was *not* my fault."

"The thing was like a damn beacon signaling that you've got money."

"Fuck you," I spat, unsure what had come over me. I'd always been taught to remain proper and composed, even in the most difficult situations.

His features remained stoic, totally unaffected by my words. "Not a chance."

My eyes widened. "You're fired."

He crossed his arms across his chest. "Some might say that's sexual harassment."

I gasped. "You're insane."

"You just fired me because I said I wouldn't sleep with you."

I could feel the heat rushing to my cheeks as my body trembled with rage. "We'll see what my parents say about this."

"Yeah, I'd love to hear what they say about their daughter propositioning an employee."

My words wouldn't come fast enough for the way I felt. "I…did *not*…proposition you."

He quirked a brow. "Didn't you?"

I spun around and stormed into my room, slamming the door behind me so the entire hallway wall rattled with the force of it.

Asshole!

CHAPTER FOUR
Kresley

My mom called the following morning after I'd just slipped on my cutoffs and T-shirt to wish me luck on my first day. I think the call was a lot less about wishing me luck and a lot more about hearing my voice. I knew it made her feel better to know I was okay. We chatted for a few minutes, but I was too embarrassed—and still pissed—to mention the encounter with my new bodyguard. But one more bad encounter and his ass was fired.

I said goodbye to my mom and threw my backpack onto my back. I stepped into the hallway and stopped short, nearly turning back around when I found Tristan against the wall in black cargo pants and a black shirt with his arms crossed.

"So much for granting requests," I grumbled as I walked toward the stairwell. Given the sound of footsteps behind me, he'd followed me.

"Nice to see you left off the jewels today," he mumbled behind me.

I said nothing, my insides twisting with so much hate I didn't know what to do with it. How could one person elicit so many negative feelings in such a short period of time? Was it his total disregard for my feelings? The fact that he pushed my buttons whenever he spoke? Or, that he thought I was high maintenance and desperate?

I stepped outside the building, instantly greeted by a thick wall of heat. I'd forgotten how warm September in

Southern California could be. I stopped on the sidewalk in front of my dorm and glanced from left to right as other students moved in all directions around me. Unfortunately, I had no idea where my first class was. I figured Marco would know, but Marco was nowhere to be found. And there wasn't a chance in hell I'd ask Tristan. I shoved my hand into my back pocket, grabbing my phone and searching my email for my schedule. It had to be there somewhere.

"It's this way," Tristan huffed, taking off to the left and onto a path that led away from the dorms toward the heart of campus.

We walked in silence as students hurried by us in a rush to get to their classes. Tristan and I didn't walk side by side up the slight incline; it was more like he followed me.

"Where's Marco?" I finally asked, not looking back for his response.

"He thought it would be better if I accompanied you to your classes. You know. Blend in more." He definitely said the last part to spite me.

"Let's get something straight," I said, stopping in the middle of the path and whirling around to face him. "You chose this job. I didn't choose this life." Since we now blocked the path, students needed to move around us to get by. "I was serious about you not working for me," I said, lowering my voice. "You clearly don't want to."

He said nothing, just stepped around me and kept walking, his head moving from side to side while he took in everyone who walked near us.

We finally reached the quad, a grassy expanse surrounded by beautiful old buildings with stone exteriors and Coral trees lining the perimeter. If I wasn't so aggravated with Tristan, I would've stopped for a minute to take in the beautiful view.

He eventually stopped outside a two-story cobblestone building. He buried his hands in his pockets, and his eyes averted mine. "You've got Communications in room 125."

"You're not coming to class with me?"

"It's already been checked. Marco's inside looking over the class roster."

Thank God for small favors. I walked past him and entered the building. Relief washed over me knowing I was away from him and his negative energy. I began to search the numbers on the plaques outside each classroom until I spotted Marco standing outside a classroom at the end of the hallway.

"You two settle your differences?" he asked as I approached.

"That was a set-up?"

He shrugged.

"I don't like him."

"He's a good man to have on your team," Marco assured me.

"He's rude."

"You don't have to like him. You just need to know he's looking out for your safety."

I didn't respond as I walked into the small classroom of no more than thirty desks. Some students were already there, so I took a seat in the center of the room. Away from the windows and away from the doors. Just inconvenient enough to give Marco time to stop any threat before it got to me.

It was sad I'd been taught things like that early on. Sad that my father's real estate business—the one that made him one of the richest real estate moguls in the world—

had caused such chaos in my life. I didn't ask to be brought up in a rich family. I didn't need the big house, fancy cars, or private jet. I just wanted to be like everyone else. But I knew as much as I wanted to be like everyone else, I wasn't. I was someone's shortcut to fortune if they could get to me. So, as long as I stayed safe, they wouldn't win.

The chatter of students around me caused me to glance around at all the unfamiliar faces in the classroom. Most of them seemed to already know each other or at least have a friend in the class. That's what happened when you transferred. You started all over again. At least I'd met Elodie and Alice who'd adopted me as their own.

I pulled up my schedule on my phone *and* a campus map. I needed to know which way to go when class ended so I didn't need to rely on Tristan. I wasn't helpless, desperate, or high maintenance. And the sooner he learned that, the sooner he and I could coexist.

***

I stepped into the hallway after class en route to my accounting class across the quad. I followed the flow of students hurrying out of the building. I knew Tristan was nearby but didn't give him the satisfaction of a glance.

"Kresley!" someone called.

My head whipped around in the direction of the voice.

"Hey," I said, grateful to see Elodie's familiar face.

"How was your first class?" she asked, walking alongside me while I assumed Tristan followed us.

"Not bad. Yours?"

"Well, as a chem major, I'm in science labs all day. So, if science is your idea of fun, it's been great."

I laughed. "Where you headed?"

She hitched her thumb toward the building to our

right. "Most of my classes are in there. But I do have a break for lunch at noon if you'd like to meet up."

"Sure. Where?"

She pointed to a building across the way with a tall flagpole in front of it. "I'll meet you inside at twelve."

"Sounds good."

We parted ways, and I made it to my accounting class with minutes to spare. Marco already stood outside the classroom.

"All clear," he said as I moved past him.

"Thanks," I said, before stepping inside the classroom. This one was bigger than my first class and had tables instead of desks with two stools at each. I took a seat at an empty table in the center of the room.

A guy with dreadlocks who smelled of patchouli oil walked over and placed his hand on the stool beside me. "Is anyone sitting here?"

I shook my head. "You are now."

He smiled as he slipped onto the stool. "I'm Jeff."

"Kresley."

"Cool name."

"Thanks."

The professor walked in. Her navy pantsuit was designer, and her shoulder-length gray hair was perfectly straight.

"I hear this class is a killer," Jeff whispered.

"*Great.*"

"I also hear there're a lot of collaborative assignments which means you may be stuck with me for the semester."

I flashed him a small smile and class began.

An hour later, my head spun with an impending headache. I struggled with math, but since accounting was a requirement, I needed to suck it up and try my best.

It wasn't like my parents were on me about my grades. Hell, they would've been happy if I stayed home and helped with my dad's business. They never pushed me to get a degree. That was what *I* wanted.

"Where you headed next?" Jeff asked as we walked out of class together.

I caught sight of Tristan out of the corner of my eye in the hallway trailing us out of the building, but again I didn't acknowledge him. "Oh, I have an hour to kill before I'm meeting my friend for lunch. How about you?"

"No class until later. You wanna chill on the quad and get some sun while you wait?"

"Oh, I…" My counselor's voice popped into my head telling me to live in the moment and not assume every person who is kind to me is out to get me. I sighed. "Sure."

He pointed to a grassy area in the corner of the quad, away from the crisscrossed paths students took to classes. "Looks like a perfect spot."

We sat down, Jeff lounging on his back using his backpack as a pillow and me tucking up my knees and wrapping my arms around them.

"So, where you from?" he asked.

I looked around the busy quad and spotted Tristan watching us as he stood under a tree in the shade. I looked back to Jeff. "California. You?"

"Montana."

"What brought you here?"

"I like exploring new places. This is my fourth college."

"No way."

He nodded. "A new school every year. At the rate I'm going, I'll be at eight before I graduate."

"Why eight?"

"Not all my credits transfer over when I start a new school. But it's no biggie. I'm in no rush to get into the real world."

I laughed, wishing I was that much of a free spirit. I'd thought I was when I packed up and left for France. But now I see that being free had just been an illusion. A foolish dream that didn't actually exist in my world.

***

At lunch with Elodie, I learned that everyone on my floor had questioned her about my bodyguards. I would've been surprised if they hadn't. She explained I was a pop star from overseas who was laying low and trying to blend in. Oddly, they bought the story *and* my need to keep my presence there quiet.

After lunch, I struggled to stay awake during special events marketing, not having slept more than a couple of hours the previous night. Once the professor dismissed us, I hurried out of the building to get back to the dorm so I could nap. The campus was less lively in the afternoon, so it gave me a chance to admire the Coral trees as I made my way toward the path leading to the dorms.

"That guy you were with," Tristan murmured from behind me once we were alone on the path. "He doesn't stay in one place for long."

"I know," I said without turning to look at him.

"He's moved around his entire life," he continued.

"So?"

"So, there's got to be a reason. People like that come with a lot of baggage which means they may be willing to do whatever it takes to make things happen."

I spun to face him, my long hair whipping over my shoulder. "I'm not sure if this is your first gig or what.

But in my world, I meet people and get to know them. I don't need a guy's dossier from you. He'll tell me what he wants me to know."

"And what if he doesn't? What if he lies about who he is?"

"Like you did at the bar?" I countered.

"I didn't lie."

"You omitted. Just as bad."

He rolled his eyes. "As I was saying, you have no idea what that guy's intentions with you are."

I scoffed. "His intentions? Who even talks like that?"

Anger brewed in his eyes. "I meant money talks. Those men who tried to—"

A girl brushed by us and Tristan stopped speaking until we were alone on the path again.

"Those men could reach out to anyone. They could offer anyone money to get close to you. Have you ever thought of that?"

"How do I know they didn't offer *you* money to pretend to be my security?"

He dropped his head back and growled. "They didn't."

"You sure? Where's your dossier?"

He didn't say anything.

"See? Sometimes you just need to trust your gut and trust people." I turned away from him and walked toward the dorm, knowing if I'd trusted my gut about *him*, I would have fired his ass for real. But I trusted Marco who'd vouched for him. And I trusted my parents who hired him because he was the best out there.

I was the one who wasn't so sure.

I was the one who needed more proof that he'd be the one I could rely on if things went south.

Because nothing so far had proven that Tristan Stone would be there if I needed him.

CHAPTER FIVE
Tristan

It was two in the morning, and I should've been asleep. But instead, I lay in bed staring at the ceiling of the damn dorm room trying to figure out how I was going to get through this fucking assignment unscathed. Because I was pretty damn sure it was gonna be the death of me.

I'd started Elite Security at eighteen. Marco came on as my partner right from the start running everything for me. He'd been Special Forces and taught me everything he knew. My plan had never been to just own the company. I knew since the age of nine that I wanted to protect those who couldn't protect themselves. And, after seven years in business, it's what I was doing.

We currently employed twenty (both in the field and working cybersecurity), but Marco wanted us to grow even bigger, opening up branches across the country. And, the only time we'd ever come to heads over something was this assignment. I knew better than to take on a young client who'd traipsed across the globe for college when she knew there could be threats against her. But Marco had stood behind his decision, arguing it was important for our expansion plans to take on high-profile clients. And it was him who promised the Hastings that he *and* I would personally handle their daughter's protection.

Fuck me.

I knew it would be bad, but *nothing* could prepare me for being at a college and protecting a rich girl who didn't give a shit about her own life. I'd called it from jump. Our typical clients hired us because they *cared* about their own safety. But this one? This one thought life as she knew it could go back to normal—back to how it had been before the botched kidnapping. Well, I had news for Miss Over-Privileged. If she expected me to do my job right, she needed to do what I said.

A door opened in the hallway. Students were constantly in and out of each other's rooms, but being late, I needed to check the live camera feeds on my monitor.

I slipped out of bed and grabbed my gun from the desk beside me. I moved to the monitor and checked the hallway feed. Kresley tiptoed down the hallway in her pajamas. *God dammit.* I moved to the door and threw it wide open. "What the fuck?"

She stopped short, turning slowly to face me. "I just needed the bathroom."

"You need to call us."

Her eyes dropped to the gun at my side and her teeth ground together. "I didn't want to bother you."

"Ironic."

She pointed at me, her index finger tapping in the air as if to poke me as hard as she could with it. "That right there is why I didn't want to call you. I didn't want to see the condescension on your face." Then, as if exhaustion had taken over her, she dropped her hand and a sigh of resignation left her. "I am trying to coexist here, but you are making it impossible."

"You keep doing careless shit," I countered, keeping my eyes on hers and not on the tiny tank top and shorts she apparently wore to bed.

"You really think someone is waiting in the bathroom for me?"

"No."

Her brows squished together. "Then what's the problem?"

"The problem is we have protocols in place for a reason."

She closed her eyes and exhaled, gesturing her hand toward the bathroom. "Go ahead."

I walked to the bathroom, pushing open the door and checking for feet under the stalls. When I saw none, I pushed open every stall door to make sure no one hid on the toilets. Then, I stepped back out into the hallway and leaned against the wall. "All clear."

Kresley walked inside.

The sweet scent of lavender body lotion wafted by me, and I couldn't help but breathe in the girlish scent. I wondered if she wore it to bed to make her sleepy since lavender had that effect. I wasn't too proud to admit I'd tried it before. Didn't work, but it was worth a shot.

The toilet flushed, and I heard the sink switch on then off. The bathroom door opened and Kresley walked out without looking at me.

"Should I expect a call in the middle of the night every night?" I asked as I followed her down the hallway.

"I don't sleep," she said, not bothering to look at me. "So probably." She stepped into her room and closed the door.

And, as I was left standing alone in the middle of the hallway at two o'clock in the fucking morning, that's when it hit me. Me and the rich princess had more in common than I realized.

Dammit.

CHAPTER SIX
Kresley

Marco standing outside my room the next morning was a welcome sight. Despite my lack of sleep the previous night and the exhaustion I currently felt, I smiled as I took in his jeans and blue Henley. "Morning."

Marco nodded, and I was beginning to realize he only spoke when absolutely necessary. Tristan was the opposite, offering his opinion freely. It must've been his age or inexperience. Because I'd been around enough bodyguards to know, they took their jobs very seriously. And pissing off the client wasn't ever their top priority.

"I like your outfit," I complimented Marco.

His lips quirked as I walked to the showers.

"You can smile, Marco," I called over my shoulder. "I won't tell my parents."

He didn't say anything, just waited outside the bathroom while I showered and then my room while I got ready for class. He walked alongside me out of the building, growling when a couple of guys pushed between us as they rushed into the dorm from what looked like their morning run.

Marco stayed a few feet behind me on the path, giving me space while still assessing the area around us. We arrived at the building where I had my Ethics class. It was more modern than the other buildings I'd been in and was located behind the library, not on the quad like my other classes. Inside, Tristan—in black on black—leaned against the hallway wall outside my classroom. I didn't meet his gaze, just said goodbye to Marco and disappeared inside.

I took a seat in the middle of the small classroom. Students filled in the seats around me and before long the professor entered and began his hour-long lecture on unethical behavior in the workplace. If ever there were a lecture Tristan needed to sit in on, this was the lecture. Luckily, it was Marco who waited for me after class. He stalled to follow me, but I slowed my pace so I could walk beside him.

We crossed campus on our way to event planning, my final class for the day.

"Watch out!" someone yelled.

Marco jumped in front of me, shielding me from impending danger. He reached out and snatched the Frisbee that flew at our heads, glaring at the guy who threw it. He tossed it back to him.

"Sorry!" the guy called.

"No problem!" I called back, trying to ease Marco's agitation while calming my own nerves. I glanced over at Marco as we continued to walk. "It would've done me some good to get knocked in the head with the Frisbee."

His forehead scrunched as he searched my face.

"A black eye would've made me look tough."

He cocked his head. "Or, like the other guy got in a good shot."

"You saying I can't protect myself?" I teased.

His eyes assessed my biceps—make that lack thereof. "You got a weapon?"

"Yeah. You."

He cracked a smile.

"There it is," I said, as much needed warmth spread to my chest. "I knew you had it in you."

* * *

"You have to tell us," Elodie whispered over dinner.

I leaned forward, inching closer to her seated across from me in the noisy dining hall. "What do you mean?"

"Who's the *other* guy?" Alice asked from beside me. "The one in the room across from yours."

I rolled my eyes on a groan. "Tristan."

"Tristan," Alice cooed.

"Don't let his good looks fool you. He's a jerk."

"I wondered about him," Elodie said. "I introduced myself as his RA and he slammed the door in my face."

"Sounds about right," I said before taking a sip of my water.

"You don't have to like him to hook up with him," Alice said, popping a French fry into her mouth. "Just tell him to keep his mouth shut."

Elodie burst out laughing.

I peeked over at Marco standing across the room and out of earshot—*thank God*. "There's no chance of that happening."

"Does that mean he's fair game?" Alice asked.

"If you're into cold jerky types," I said.

"I'm into *his* type. He's got to be the hottest guy on campus," she said.

I wouldn't argue with that. Those eyes *were* hypnotizing, but… "Just be warned," I said. "The second he opens his mouth, he'll ruin it for you."

CHAPTER SEVEN
Tristan

I lay in bed staring up at the ceiling, my nightly routine as I waited for Kresley's two a.m. bathroom run. Sleep felt heavy in my eyes, but I fought it. It was just a matter of time before I got her text anyway.

I glanced to the desk. The live camera feeds on the monitor displayed the hallway, exits, basement, and stairwells. The dark one was for Kresley's room. I climbed out of bed and stood in front of the monitor. It was forbidden to check her room unless we had reason to do so. But if I just peeked to see if she was asleep, I could attempt to get some sleep of my own. *As if that would be a pleasant experience.*

I knew it was wrong, but I switched on the camera feed anyway. What I didn't expect to find was Kresley pacing the floor. Our cameras were state-of-the-art and high-definition, so there was no denying what I was seeing. She'd told me she didn't sleep. I just thought she was being dramatic.

I watched the camera feed for at least ten minutes and not once did she stop pacing. She paced in a straight line. Then she switched it up and walked in a circle. Was she trying to put herself to sleep? Was she scared to close her eyes? I wondered if her insomnia began before or after Paris. *Hold up.* It wasn't my responsibility to figure out why she wasn't sleeping. It was my responsibility to protect her.

I closed my eyes and pinched the bridge of my nose. Now that I knew she didn't sleep, was I supposed to do something with that information? Was I supposed to tell Marco? And, how would that conversation go? 'Hey, Marco, while totally disregarding protocol and switching on Kresley's camera feed, I saw she doesn't sleep.'

Yeah. No, thanks.

A text pinged on my phone.

I opened my eyes and checked my screen. **Bathroom**

I quickly switched off the feed to her room, as if she could somehow sense I had it on, and moved to the door. I opened it at the same time Kresley opened her door. She walked out without saying a word, unaware that I'd been watching her. She moved down the hallway, waiting outside the bathroom, knowing the drill. I moved past her, checking it and walking out a minute later. "All clear."

I leaned against the hallway wall while she took care of business. When she stepped back out, I followed her to her room. She opened the door and moved inside.

"Hey," I said, stopping her before she closed the door.

She glanced back to me, her red eyes indicating her need for sleep.

"Do you want me to sit out here tonight?" *What the fuck was I doing?*

She tilted her head. "In the hallway?"

I shrugged. "Just thought it might give you peace of mind."

She shook her head. "I'm fine." She turned and closed her door, leaving me standing alone in the empty hallway. And, despite her usual show of bravado, she was far from fine.

I moved back inside my room, and against my better judgment, I flipped on her room feed. Call it curiosity. Call it me calling her bluff. But I proceeded to watch her pace her floor until five in the morning when the sun began to rise and she finally slipped into bed.

There was no way she could continue going to school during the day and staying up all night. She'd eventually break, and that would be on me. Because, while I shouldn't know she didn't sleep, I was the only one who fucking *knew* she didn't sleep.

God dammit!

Kresley

Not sleeping at night was beginning to wear on me, so when Elodie and Alice invited me to a frat party Friday night, I was all in. Drinks and partying would definitely wear me out. Then I'd sleep. Nightmares be damned. I informed Marco about the plan to go to the party, and he instantly took off for the frat house. I pitied the frat guys who had to deal with him.

When it was time to get ready, I slipped on some skinny jeans, a sleeveless navy top, and nude Louboutin heels. I curled my hair in loose waves, brushed on some blush and eye shadow, and swiped a pass of gloss across my lips.

Around nine, there was a knock on my door.

"It's us!" Elodie and Alice announced at the same time.

I smiled and opened the door to find them both giggling.

"Are you two already drunk?" I asked.

Alice shook her head while Elodie nodded. Though amusing, it was their big eyes that told me there was more to their giddy behavior.

I stuck my head out into the hallway. Tristan stood against the wall in black on black staring down at his phone. Now I understood what caused their behavior. "Looks like our escort is ready," I said to them as I slipped into the hallway. I heard Tristan push off the wall and follow us out of the building.

Once outside, the girls led the way down the sidewalk.

"Woah," Tristan said.

We all stopped, turning to look at him behind us.

"You're not walking," he said.

"It looks like we're walking," I said.

He looked to Elodie and Alice. "I've got a car."

"He's got a car," Alice said all giddy at the thought of riding in a vehicle with him.

"It's nice of you to offer," I said. "But I'm good with walking."

"Get in the car," he said, sounding pissed.

"I'm sorry. I think you've mistaken me for someone else," I said, now that he thought he was going to dole out orders in front of other people.

"Nope," he shot back. "Same high maintenance princess from the bar."

I sucked in a sharp breath as my blood began to boil. It was one thing to do this in private, but to do it in front of my new friends pissed me off. I stood tall, pulling my shoulders back. "Well, since I'm the boss and am not *desperate* for a ride, this is how it's going to play out. I'm going to walk with my friends to a frat party where I plan to get pretty damn drunk. You are more than welcome to follow us there. Or, you can drive the car and meet us there which would probably be welcome later when we can no longer stand up straight. Your call."

He glared across the space between us, the ticking in his jaw throbbing like the second hand on an old clock.

"Looks like it's settled." I spun around, linked my arms with the girls, and walked toward the frat.

"Damn, girl," Alice whispered. "That was hot."

"Hot?" I asked quietly.

"The two of you," Elodie answered.

I groaned and they both laughed as they directed me toward the frat house. It took a good ten minutes to get there with Tristan trailing a few feet behind us. Note to self. Take the ride next time.

Music pounded the pavement beneath our feet as we neared the two-story white house. Lights poured out the black shuttered windows and Greek letters flanked the peak of the roof. From the street, it looked like a packed house.

We walked up the sidewalk and into the open front door. People filled the rooms, and Elodie and Alice waved to those who called out to them. I followed them to the end of the hallway to a door leading downstairs. As soon as we stepped into the basement, we found the source of the loud music and people dancing under the glow of black lights.

"Come on," Elodie called, leading us to the bar. She must have known the guy running the keg because they chatted briefly, and he got us three cups of beer pretty quickly. We held up our red cups and tapped them together.

"To a wild night," I said.

"To a wild night," they repeated with excitement in their eyes.

I tipped back my cup and drained the contents.

"You weren't kidding," Alice said once I finished.

I shook my head as I wiped my mouth with the back of my hand. "I plan to get very drunk."

They held up their cups and cheered like I'd done something so much better than chugged my beer.

"It's been a hell of a first week, and I haven't really slept. I need something to help me along."

Elodie tipped back her cup and downed her beer. "Can't let a girl get drunk by herself."

I laughed as Alice did the same.

The guy by the keg refilled our cups, and we made our way out onto the dance floor, flailing our arms to the music. We danced to the next few songs and drained our cups.

I sensed someone watching me and turned to my right. A good-looking guy with dark hair and a sexy smirk stared at me. I smiled at him and that's all it took. He walked out onto the dance floor, moving behind me and placing his hands on my hips. He moved right along with my body to the beat of the song. "I'm Chris," he said, leaning in with his lips beside my ear.

"Kresley."

"You're beautiful," he said.

Heat pulsed in my cheeks as I continued dancing, not minding the feel of Chris' hands on my hips at all. It had been a long time since I'd been in a guy's arms, and I was long overdue.

Elodie and Alice's eyes were all big—the way they'd been when they saw Tristan in the hallway earlier.

Speaking of Tristan.

I glanced around the crowded space and spotted him almost immediately. He was taller than most and was leaning against the bar, staring at me with his arms crossed. His lips were pressed into a tight line and annoyance played in his eyes.

The song switched to a slow one, and I was all too happy to break eye contact with Tristan. I turned to face Chris, noting how dark his eyes were in such close proximity. The complete opposite of Tristan's. "One more song?" I asked.

Chris smiled as I draped my arms over his shoulders. He wrapped his arms around my hips and rested his hands above my ass. "I've never seen you before," he said, his eyes staring into mine. "Are you new here?"

I nodded. "I just transferred."

"Lucky me," he said.

I laughed as we moved to the slow tempo of the music.

"What year are you?" he asked.

"Senior. You?"

"Do you have a problem with younger guys?" he asked.

"Not at all."

"Thank God." He exaggerated a sigh of relief. "I'm a junior."

I laughed, loving the easy flow of our conversation.

The song eventually ended and a fast one began.

"Let me get you another drink," Chris said before leading me to the bar—the opposite end from where Tristan still stood. The bartender saw Chris and handed over two beers.

"Do you live in the frat?" I asked as we drank our beers away from the crowded dance floor.

"Yeah. You wanna see my room? I got the huge corner room."

"Um…" A cold sweat swept over me. It was a harmless question. Why was I getting so nervous about the idea of being alone with him?

"It's okay," he said, sensing my hesitation. "Maybe another time."

I nodded, appreciating that he wasn't pushing me. "Yeah. Another time."

He ticked his head toward the dance floor. "I see your friends. Let's go show them how it's done."

We joined Elodie and Alice back on the dance floor.

The party began to thin out after one. Elodie motioned toward the stairs. "You ready?"

"Yeah." I was exhausted and drunk. I couldn't wait to slip under my covers because I was going to sleep so well.

"Let me get your number," Chris said.

I rattled it off as he punched it into his phone, then he walked us upstairs and toward the front door. For the first time, he noticed Tristan following us.

"Hey man? Who you here with?" Chris asked him.

"I'm with them," Tristan said, though his eyes were on mine.

Chris looked to me, his brows knit together. "Is he?"

"He's Alice's older brother," I lied.

Alice gasped.

"He's very overprotective and insists on following us everywhere," I explained.

Chris looked to Tristan who didn't seem amused by my explanation.

"Well…" I paused awkwardly by the open front door. This was usually where the guy went in for the kiss. But Chris and I had three sets of eyes on us. The girls knew enough to hang back and pretend not to be staring, but Tristan kept walking, brushing between us on his way outside so Chris and I needed to step away from each other. "It was fun hanging out tonight," I said to Chris, trying to ignore Tristan's rude behavior.

"Yeah, it was," Chris agreed.

"See you around," I said before stepping outside with the girls following.

"Marco dropped off the SUV," Tristan informed us as soon as we were away from the front door. "It's behind the house."

Alice and Elodie eagerly followed him. I trailed behind, not wanting to seem too *desperate* to give in to his wishes to drive us. But, I was walking sideways, so out of necessity, it was safer to take the ride.

The girls slipped into the backseat first. I used my hip to push Alice into the middle of the backseat.

"You should've kissed him," Alice said.

"Totally," Elodie agreed.

"I wasn't feeling the audience," I explained as Tristan floored it in reverse out of the parking spot, sending the three of us tipping sideways—purposely, no doubt. It didn't matter, we broke into drunken laughter anyway as we righted ourselves.

Elodie looked past Alice to me. "Are you gonna see Chris again?"

"Maybe."

"He was in my chem class last year," Elodie explained. "He's a really good guy."

Tristan made a low, choked sound in the front seat.

"Was that a scoff?" I asked Tristan.

"Just a tickle in my throat, ma'am," he said.

Ma'am? Son of a bitch.

"Did *you* have fun tonight?" I asked him. "Because by the looks of it, you were having a ball holding up that bar."

"Oh, yeah. Like totally fun," he deadpanned.

"Did you get any phone numbers?" I asked.

"Tons," he lied. At least, I assumed he lied.

"Too bad," I said.

His eyes met mine in the rearview mirror.

"Once you open your mouth, they'll realize how mean you are," I explained.

He scoffed.

"That was definitely a scoff," I said.

"Definitely," Alice and Elodie agreed.

"Can you all just focus on not throwing up in the car?" he said, dismissing us with his tone of voice.

"I'm not feeling sick. How about you girls?" I said looking between Elodie and Alice.

"Nope," Alice said.

"Not me," Elodie agreed.

"See?" I met his eyes in the mirror again. "Nothing to worry about back here, sir."

Tristan eventually pulled to a stop in front of our dorm and killed the engine.

The three of us tumbled out of the backseat giggling. We unsteadily climbed the stairs to the second floor then said goodbye in the hallway. The two of them fell into their room and burst into laughter. "Night, Kresley!"

"Night," I called as I made my way to my room.

Tristan brushed by me, unlocking my door, and checking my room. He stepped back into the hallway.

I could sense him looking at me, so I shifted my gaze to meet his. "What?"

He shook his head as if he had nothing to say in that judgmental brain of his. But I knew he did.

"It's okay for me to have fun," I said. "You don't have to try to make me feel guilty for it."

He buried his hands in his pockets. "Not what I'm doing."

"And just because a guy wanted to spend the night dancing with me doesn't make me desperate."

"Why are you telling me this?"

"Because I hate that stupid condescending look you give me. Like you think you're so much better than me. It sucks."

He didn't say anything. He just stared at me.

"And I just thought you should know." I walked inside my room and slammed the door behind me, hating how riled up he made me. Why did I care what he thought?

I pulled off my clothes and slipped into bed in my underwear and bra without brushing my teeth or washing up. I could feel sleep near, and no judgmental bodyguard with a chip on his shoulder was going to keep me from it.

CHAPTER EIGHT
Tristan

I dropped down onto the edge of my bed and dragged my fingers through my hair. What a fucking night. Was this the sort of thing this job would entail? Watching the client meet guys and get drunk? *Really?*

And, did she have to be so damn stubborn all the time? She wouldn't let me drive them to the party when I knew how exhausted she had to be. She was burning the candle at both fucking ends. But instead of taking my generosity for what it was, she had to go accuse me of giving her orders. Why was she hell-bent on proving she was tough? It was infuriating.

My eyes drifted to the monitor on the desk. Both the entrances, stairwells, hallway, and basement camera feeds were on. I swore I wouldn't check her room feed again. But the damn vision of her pacing around her room— and the knowledge that I was the only one who knew— clawed away at my insides.

Fuuuuuuuck.

I pushed myself to my feet and moved to the monitor. I stared at the dark square for a long time, begging myself not to do it. But my curiosity won out. I switched it on, breathing a sigh of relief when I found her sound asleep in bed. My finger lingered over the off button, but instead, I zoomed in on her face. Her eyelashes touched the tips of her cheeks. Her lips were puckered. She looked so innocent and fragile while she slept—the complete opposite of the fierce, feisty girl I had to deal with.

I wondered which was the real Kresley Hastings. And, if I'd ever really find out.

* * *

A text pinged on my phone, pulling me from a sound sleep. I cracked my eyes open, noting the sunlight filtering into my room as I reached over and grabbed my phone off the desk. I checked the screen. **Bathroom.**

I climbed out of bed and opened the door. Kresley stood against the hallway wall across from me. Her eyes widened before darting away from me. I glanced down. I was only in my boxers. *Ah, well.* I walked into the hallway and knocked on the bathroom door.

"Hold on!" a girl called.

Kresley and I stood awkwardly in the hallway, me in my boxers and her avoiding me like the plague.

"All set," the girl said as she slipped out of the bathroom. She drank in my bare chest before darting into a nearby room.

Kresley scoffed low in her throat, and it took everything in me not to give her shit for questioning my scoff the previous night. Instead, I entered the bathroom, did a quick sweep, and walked back out.

Kresley moved around me and slipped inside, stepping back out a short time later and dodging my eyes. "I'm grabbing breakfast with the girls in ten minutes."

"Marco's on today."

"Please let him know." With that, she hurried back to her room and disappeared inside before I could even check it.

What happened to the drunk princess from the previous night? Did she regret the way she'd spoken to me or did she not even remember?

Kresley

I stood with my back pressed against my closed door, my heart racing a mile a minute. Holy mother of all things sacred. Why in the world did he need to be shirtless? And, why did he have to be all jacked underneath his clothes? *Holy six-pack, Batman.* It was like the moment I first saw him all over again. My brain became all frazzled by his presence. His eyes. That voice. The same hum of electricity coasted over my skin.

There was a knock on my door and I jumped.

"Kresley?" Elodie called. "You ready?"

My entire body deflated, betraying me on so many levels. What was wrong with me? I didn't want it to be my moody bodyguard. I couldn't stand him. I pulled myself together and opened the door.

Alice and Elodie stood there with toothy grins on their faces.

"What's up with you two?"

"You tell us," Elodie said.

They pushed past me into my room. I shut the door and turned to face them now both sitting on my bed, anticipation lighting up their eyes.

"What happened after we left you two alone last night?" Elodie asked.

"What do you mean what happened?"

"Did he walk you inside your room?" Alice asked.

"No."

"Did he try to kiss you?" Elodie asked.

"*No.*"

"Then what happened?" they asked at the same time.

"First of all, it's like you two share a brain. And second, nothing happened. I told him he sucked. Then I went to bed."

"It's gonna happen," Alice said.

"What?"

"You and him," Elodie explained.

"Why would you say that?" I asked, now curious since I'd had another "reaction" to him.

"He's not fair game anymore," Alice said. "I'm bowing out gracefully."

"What? You're crazy."

She shook her head. "There's so much sexual tension between the two of you, you can almost feel it."

"I just can't wait to see who caves first," Elodie added.

CHAPTER NINE
Kresley

I slipped on jeans and a T-shirt, twisted my hair into a high ponytail, and slipped on my shoes, ready for another Monday. My phone rang as soon as I opened my door. Tristan stood waiting. I stopped in the doorway and answered the call. "Hey, Mom," I said, having seen her name on the screen. "I'm just on my way out to class."

"Did you order something and have it sent to the house?" she asked with urgency in her tone.

"What?"

"Did you order something and have it sent here?" she demanded.

I thought for a second, but knew I hadn't. "No. Why?"

"A package just arrived and it's addressed to you," she explained.

"Where's it from?"

"There's no return address," she said.

I could hear voices in the background. "Stand back, Mrs. Hastings."

My heartbeat sped up. "Mom?"

Silence.

"Mom, are you there?" I nearly cried as Tristan pushed off the wall with concern on his face.

"Put it on speaker," he said urging me into my room.

I switched it on speaker as I stepped back into my room and sat on the edge of my bed, listening for confirmation that she was okay.

"Yes," my mother finally said. "I'm here. I'm just staying back while security checks it."

"What is it?" I asked, fearing it was an explosive.

"Hold on," she whispered.

"Just stay back, Mom," I said as tears glazed my eyes and fear grabbed hold of me. I stared at Tristan, watching for his reaction.

"Oh, my God," she said, her breath leaving her in a relieved sigh.

"What?"

"It's a bottle of perfume," she explained, almost laughing.

"I didn't order perfume," I said.

"What kind is it?" she asked her security.

"It's French," one of them said.

My mother gasped.

My stomach dropped.

"Mrs. Hastings, this is Tristan. Is there a note?"

"There's no note," she said.

My pulse began to drum in my ears and my hands began to tremble.

"You need to come home," my mother said.

A million thoughts whirled through my brain. They knew where I lived. This wasn't over. It was just a matter of time before they found me. "Mom, whoever sent the perfume sent it to our *home*. They clearly don't know where I am. I think for the time being I'm safer here."

"Have the police been called?" Tristan asked.

"They're already on their way," my mother explained.

"Good," Tristan said. "Have security get that package out of your house."

"Take that outside," she ordered them.

"The police will need to check that package for bugs, tracking devices, and explosives."

She sighed.

"Don't worry, Mrs. Hastings. We've got things covered here. But your security needs to be on high alert."

"Please keep my baby safe," my mother said as if I wasn't right there.

He locked eyes with me. "You have my word."

Tristan and I may have had our differences, but there was something about his assurance to my mother that made me believe he would protect me.

Tristan

I paced the hallway outside Kresley's afternoon class, checking the stairwell and monitoring her social media newsfeed—the one that made it appear as if she transferred to school in New York. She'd been right when she told her mother she was safer here. She was. Marco and I wouldn't let anything happen to her, especially now that the threat level had moved from potential to imminent.

The classroom door swung open at three on the dot. The professor stepped into the hallway and hurried toward the building exit like he always did, in a rush to get to his next class across campus. The students filed out next. I watched each of them leave, walking down the hallway to the exit—some talking to classmates, some with their eyes on their phones, and others with their ear pods in.

My eyes shifted from side to side.

Alarm bells wailed in my head.

Where's Kresley?

I rushed to the open classroom door, freezing as I stepped inside.

Kresley's head was down on her desk, her left cheek resting on her arms and her blonde waves spread out all over the desk.

She was asleep.

Just like on the monitor, her eyelashes brushed the tips of her pink cheeks. A soft sigh escaped her lips and she looked so damn peaceful. Had the news of the package wiped her out? Had she felt safer sleeping in a room full of strangers than sleeping in a room by herself?

I glanced to the desk beside hers, contemplating if I should sit. Instead, I switched off the bright classroom lights and grabbed the doorknob, closing the door quietly.

In the empty hallway, I sat down on the floor against the wall. She needed the sleep, and no one seemed to need the classroom. I wondered what Marco would say if he found out I let her sleep. Would he give me shit for ignoring protocol? Would he question my motives? If it were the other way around, there was no doubt in my mind that I'd question his.

Kresley

I jerked awake, my head springing up off the desk. *The desk?* My eyes shot around the dark empty classroom. How long had I been asleep? I snatched my belongings off the floor and stood, rushing to the classroom door. I threw it open and stepped into the hallway, nearly tripping over someone sitting on the floor outside. "Oh my God."

Tristan looked up at me, his eyes softer than normal.

"What are you doing?" I asked, my voice echoing in the deserted hallway.

"Waiting for you."

"Why didn't you wake me? How long have I been asleep? What time is it?"

He pushed himself to his feet. Since he was a foot taller than me, I had to tip my head back to meet those teal eyes. "You clearly needed to sleep. It's almost six."

My eyes widened. "Six? Why'd you let me sleep that long?"

Indecision flashed across his eyes as they riveted between mine.

"What?" I asked.

He shook his head, clearly keeping something from me.

"I'm not going anywhere until you tell me."

He arched a brow. "You gonna stomp your foot, too?"

I stomped my foot.

He snorted. "So, what is this? A standoff?"

His question made my statement sound ridiculous, but I'd said it, so now I needed to own it. "Yes."

"Well, I've got all night." He sat back down on the floor.

Was he really doing this? Was *I* really doing this? *Damn him.*

I sat down on the dusty floor a good three feet away from him.

A stretch of silence passed between us.

Too many questions rushed through my brain. What was he keeping from me? Had he heard more about the package? Why had he let me sleep? Why were we sitting in an empty hallway in the midst of a standoff? "Have you heard anything more about the package?"

He shook his head.

"Do you think they'll find me here?"

He shrugged.

I huffed, hating his silent answers. "Tell me why you let me sleep."

"You told me you don't sleep," he finally admitted. "I figured you needed it, especially after what happened earlier."

"I sleep. I just sleep better during the day."

"Why not at night? Marco and I are right there."

I knew they were and wished it was enough. But it wasn't. I shrugged.

"Would it help if I stayed outside your door?" he asked.

The kindness in his tone was disconcerting. Just like when he'd offered to sit outside my room once before. It was out of character for him. Did he really care that I had trouble sleeping? Or, was he just doing his job? "I can't ask you to do that."

"Of course you can. I work for you, remember?"

My forehead creased. "Are you throwing my words back in my face?"

"Just stating the truth."

I didn't reply, hating that he was so hard to read. One minute he was being kind. The next his condescension seemed to be rearing its ugly head. But did it really matter? I didn't need to be able to read him. I only needed him to keep me safe—now more than ever. "Maybe you can just bring me to the liquor store."

His head hitched back. "The liquor store?"

"I tend to sleep after I've been drinking."

"Your dad will just love it when you come home for Thanksgiving an alcoholic."

I smirked. "I'll just blame you."

He chuckled.

The unfamiliar sound of his brief laughter caused a flutter inside my chest. And, instead of being annoyed that he may have been mocking me, his reaction resonated something warm inside of me.

Maybe I'd been wrong about Tristan.

Maybe I didn't know him at all.

CHAPTER TEN
Tristan

The urge to check Kresley's camera feed taunted me. After what happened this morning and her falling asleep in class, I needed to know if she was pacing the floor. But I needed to follow the rules *I'd* created.

I checked my phone. It was just after one. I moved to my door, hoping to God I wasn't making a monumental mistake. I twisted the knob so I didn't make any noise and tiptoed across the hall. The idiot next door to me had his rap music playing making it impossible to hear anything, so I pressed my ear to Kresley's door. If Marco was looking at the hallway feed, I'd have a lot of explaining to do. But it took no more than a couple of seconds to hear footsteps inside. I tapped lightly on her door.

Silence.

Good girl. Never ask who it is, especially in the middle of the night. "Kresley. It's Tristan," I whispered.

Her footsteps moved to the door, but she didn't open it. "How do I know?"

"Know what?" I whispered.

"That it's really you."

She seemed to be making a habit out of seeing how far she could push me. "What the fuck," I grumbled.

Her door swung open. "It's definitely you."

My eyes moved over the tight tank top and tiny pajama shorts she wore. She must've caught me looking because she crossed her arms across her chest. I met her eyes, cursing myself for forgetting myself. I'd seen beautiful girls before in far less. "I just wanted to let you know I was gonna sit out here for a bit."

Irritation flittered across her eyes. "I told you it's unnecessary."

"And I'm telling you I'm gonna sit out here anyway."

Her eyes dropped to the floor, her stubbornness wavering. She knew, like I did, that it could help her sleep. Extended sleep deprivation did strange things to your psyche. So did fear. She knew it. And I knew it. We also both knew that when it came to our rocky relationship, something needed to give. Reluctantly, she nodded.

"Good night," I said, grabbing her doorknob.

She stepped back into her room and I closed the door, lowering myself down to the floor and leaning against the door. I hoped having me there helped her sleep. Because I knew all too well that not sleeping was a real son of a bitch.

Kresley

I didn't get into bed. Instead, I sat on the floor with my back against my door. There wasn't a doubt in my mind that Tristan would sit there all night, and the unexpected—and uninvited—fluttering in my stomach wouldn't let me leave him just yet.

"How did you know I was awake?" I asked through the door.

He huffed. "I heard you pacing. Now get in bed."

I laughed, his bossiness not as intimidating at one in the morning through a door.

"I'm serious. Get in bed."

"Be careful. Some girls like bossy guys."

"What the fuck?" he grumbled, and I heard his head fall back against the door with a thump.

I suppressed my laughter, really beginning to like pushing his buttons. "Fine. I'll get in bed. But promise me Marco's on duty tomorrow."

"Why?"

"Because if you stay up all night outside my door, you need to sleep."

"It's not your job to worry about me," he said.

"Then whose job is it?"

A long silence passed. He wasn't going to answer my question. And, suddenly, I wanted to know the answer. Did he have a girlfriend waiting for him back home wherever he lived? Did he have parents who called to check on him like mine called to check on me? Did he have friends he texted just to check in?

It was late, and I wanted to see if I'd actually sleep with him out there, so I took his kindness for what it was and stood up. I pressed my hands to the door. "Good night, Tristan. Thank you for this."

He didn't reply, which I expected.

I moved to my bed and climbed under my comforter. I gave the soft lights wrapped around my room one last look then closed my eyes.

It took no time before sleep pulled me under.

CHAPTER ELEVEN
Kresley

I stepped into the hallway after the first good night sleep I'd had since arriving to Remington. Marco waited for me. And, though I told Tristan not to be there, I still couldn't ignore the unexpected tinge of disappointment inside me. "Morning, Marco."

"Ma'am."

I stopped, pegging him with my eyes. "Marco, I will hurt you if you don't call me by my name."

"Ma'am, at this point I just do it to piss you off," he deadpanned.

I burst out laughing and started down the hall. "I appreciate your humor, Marco."

We made it downstairs and walked across campus toward my first class.

"You missed a good party Friday night," I teased him.

"I'm a little old for frat parties," he said.

"Would you prefer I join the chess club?"

"That would put me to sleep."

We reached my building and climbed the steps. "I can't win with you."

He chuckled as we entered the building and approached my class. I walked inside, leaving him behind with a quick wave of my hand.

Tristan

The sound of my phone ringing jolted me from a deep sleep. With my eyes closed, I felt around for my phone on the desk, grabbing it and lifting it to my ear. "Yeah?"

"We need to talk," Marco said, sounding pissed.

"Then talk."

"What was last night about?"

"What do you mean?" I asked, turning onto my side and realizing the sun was shining brightly through my blinds. I glanced at the time. Nine thirty. What the hell? I'd only gotten a few hours of sleep.

"Sitting outside her room," Marco continued. "That's not protocol."

"She doesn't sleep at night. She paces her floor all fucking night."

He didn't say anything, and I hoped to God he didn't question how I knew.

"I told her I'd sit there so maybe it would help her sleep, especially since she was still worried about the package and all."

Silence continued to fill his end for a long stretch. "Promise me that's all it is," he demanded.

"That's all it is," I assured him.

"I'll have to fire your ass if it's something else."

"I own the company. So, no, you won't fire my ass."

"You put me in charge. You swore to follow the same rules in the field as everyone else."

He was right. I had. "I just wanted to help her sleep. That's all," I explained.

Again, silence filled his end. "Fine," he finally said, before ending the call.

I tossed my phone down. Fire my ass? He was delusional. Me sitting outside her room had helped. I hadn't heard a single footstep all night long. And I was the reason why.

Kresley

Since I'd missed dinner with Elodie and Alice the previous night, I met up with them for dinner. Elodie glanced to Marco who stood in his normal spot off to the side and out of earshot. "Where's Mr. Hottie tonight?"

"I told him to take today off. He did something for me last night, and I knew he'd be tired."

They both leaned in, their eyes wide. "What?"

I laughed. "Not tired because of *that.*"

"Damn," Alice said. "I was hoping for something juicy."

"I was hoping one of you caved," Elodie added.

I shook my head, ever amused by the two of them.

After dinner, I went back to my room to finish homework then I turned on a movie. A few minutes into it, my phone pinged with a text. I grabbed it from beside me.

Hey, Kresley. It's Chris. Remember me?

I smiled as I responded to his text. **Chris? Refresh my memory.**

The bouncing dots began. Then his text appeared. **Hottest guy at the party Friday night.**

I laughed to myself. **Hmmmmm. It's not clicking.**

His response came quick. **Hell of a dancer.**

Me: Were you the one dancing on the bar?

Chris: Come on. You know who I am.

Me: Lol.

Chris: I ended up going home for the rest of the weekend. Sorry I didn't text sooner.

Me: Why are you sorry?
Chris: I would've liked to see you.

I smiled, remembering how much fun we had together Friday night. Spending time with Chris was easy. And I certainly needed a little easy in my life when everything else was so complicated. **I'm not going anywhere.**

Chris: Not true. You're going to dinner with me Friday night.

I considered the hoops he'd have to jump through to take me out. My security would have to do a background check, secure the restaurant ahead of time, and follow us on our date. **You sure you're up for that?**

Chris: Why wouldn't I be?

I laughed to myself. I hadn't considered that I'd have to tell him I had security and all that came with it. But I was twenty-one and pretty damn lonely. So, I responded the way a college girl should respond when asked out by a really nice guy. **Sure. Sounds good.**

Chris: Do you like Italian food?
Me: Yes.
Chris: Then we'll go to Fabian's. They've got really good food.
Me: Great. What time?
Chris: 7
Me: I'm in Gorham Hall. I'll meet you out front at 7.
Chris: Can't wait!

I placed my phone down beside me. Was I making a huge mistake going out with Chris? Would Marco and Tristan be pissed they'd have extra work to do to prepare for my date? I really needed to stop worrying about inconveniencing them. What was the alternative? Stay locked up like a princess in a castle for fear of troubling them? I hadn't been lying when I told Tristan that I deserved to have fun. Because I did.

I finished the movie then checked the time on my phone. Midnight. I glanced to my door and noticed the shadow beneath it. A sense of relief washed over me as I climbed under my comforter and closed my eyes, knowing a good night sleep was near.

CHAPTER TWELVE
Kresley

I slipped into a red wrap dress Friday night that tied on the side. I curled my hair into loose waves and brushed on minimal makeup. I'd had a long meeting with Marco after he did the background check on Chris. He promised to stay out of sight in the restaurant if he could drive us. I wasn't sure how Chris would feel about having a "driver," but he agreed. I sort of left off the part that he was actually my bodyguard, telling him only that my parents were crazy overprotective and insisted that I have a driver.

I checked my phone. Five to seven. I grabbed my silver clutch and headed into the hallway. Marco stood there in his black outfit.

"Hi," I said. "Thanks so much for doing this. I know it probably took some time to set up."

"It's my job, ma'am." He looked me up and down respectfully. "You look nice."

I clutched my heart. "A compliment? To what do I owe this honor?"

"Smartass," he grumbled before walking me down the stairs and outside. The car was parked at the curb with Tristan in the driver's seat.

I looked to Marco. "Wait. You're not coming?"

He shook his head. "Tristan's on tonight."

My heartbeat sped up. This wasn't how I envisioned the date playing out. Tristan was bound to do or say something to ruin the night. I just knew it. And, that

sucked because we were just getting to a better place—
at least *I* thought we were. He was sitting outside my
room, for God's sake. "But I thought…"

Marco stared at me, waiting for me to finish my
thought.

I didn't.

"Have a nice night," he said as he turned and walked
back into the building.

"Kresley," Chris called.

I spun around to find him walking toward me on the
sidewalk. He was wearing khaki pants and a blue button-
down shirt.

I smiled. "Hi."

He glanced to the car. "Is this our ride?"

I nodded.

"Does he open the door for us?" he asked,
conspiratorially.

"No." I went to open the back door knowing there
was no way in hell Tristan was about to open the door
for us, but Chris nudged me out of the way so he could
open it for me.

"Allow me."

I scooted in first.

Chris followed me in, closing the door as he did.
"Nice ride." He took in the interior of the car before he
settled his eyes on me. "You look beautiful."

Heat pulsed in my cheeks, partly because I knew
Tristan—the same Tristan who'd sat outside my door all
night long to slay the demons in my dreams—could hear
everything being said. "Thanks."

Tristan pulled away from the sidewalk with a slight
jerk, driving us toward the restaurant without a word.

"So, you mentioned you went home for the
weekend," I said to Chris. "Where's home?"

"Clayville. About an hour from here. It was my grandmother's birthday."

"Awww. How old is she?"

"Eighty-five. But you'd never guess it by the way she loves to dance," he said. "She had us all dancing around her kitchen."

I smiled. "Well, you *are* a hell of a dancer. You had to get it from somewhere."

He laughed. "Where're you from?"

"Atherton."

His eyes widened, probably because most people from California knew it was one of the wealthiest areas in the state. I immediately wanted to retract my answer, realizing I may have been offering up too much information. But it was too late. "You said you transferred here, right?"

I nodded.

"Where'd you go before this?" he asked.

I met Tristan's eyes in the rearview mirror. I knew he was waiting to hear what I'd tell Chris. But I wasn't stupid. I'd told Elodie and Alice about France because I had two security guards living around me and following me everywhere. There was no avoiding that conversation. But since I didn't know if I'd even see Chris after tonight, vague would have to work—so would deflection. "Overseas. But the food was terrible. Speaking of food. I've never been to Fabian's. Tell me what's good."

And just like that, the conversation had been averted.

* * *

Our conversation over dinner flowed easily. Thankfully, Tristan didn't come into the restaurant. But, from time to time, I could see him through the front window pacing on the sidewalk in his dark clothes.

"So, have your parents always been overprotective?" Chris asked as he ate his chicken parmesan.

"You could say that. But I know it's because they love me. You know, better safe than sorry. So, if I can put their minds at ease, I do it."

"Are you an only child?"

I nodded as I took a bite of my chicken marsala.

"Well, that explains it."

I laughed. If he only knew.

"Do you like Remington so far?"

"Everyone seems really nice. Even youngsters like yourself," I teased before sipping my glass of wine.

"*Heeeeey.*"

I smiled.

We finished up dinner a little while later and Chris paid the bill. Tristan was back in the driver's seat of the car when we stepped outside.

"Do you need to get back now or can we go somewhere else?" Chris asked.

"What were you thinking?"

"I saw a sign for an open mic night."

"Do you sing?"

"Sing?" He laughed. "Not even a little. But it could be fun to watch other people."

I hadn't anticipated a second location when I told Marco where we were going. Tristan was not going to like it. But it wasn't about him. It was about me. And I was having a nice time with Chris, so I wouldn't allow it to end just because I was scared of what my bodyguard would say. "Sure."

Chris opened the car door for me and once I slipped into the backseat, he followed me in.

"Tristan?" I said, meeting his eyes in the rearview mirror. "We're thinking of heading to an open mic night."

His eyes narrowed, pissed at the unexpected change in plans. He looked at Chris. "Where is it?"

"Just down the road a couple of miles," Chris explained, rattling off a few directions.

Tristan started the engine and followed Chris' directions. I could tell he was mad, and I couldn't stop the guilt from creeping inside me.

"Why'd you need to ask him?" Chris asked. "Doesn't he just drive wherever you tell him to?"

I could sense Tristan's eyes on me, so I avoided that rearview mirror. "Just common courtesy."

Chris nodded, my response a good enough answer for him.

We arrived at the bar where the open mic night was. Through the glass windows, it appeared dark inside but the bright neon signs in the windows practically lit up the block.

"Just give me a minute," Tristan said, as he stepped out of the car and slammed the door behind him, clearly not happy about having to check the place out first.

"What does that mean?" Chris asked me.

"He's probably just checking that it's not too crowded before he leaves us here," I said, trying to brush it off as normal. "So, if you can't sing, maybe you can get up there and recite some poetry or maybe do a magic trick. What do you think?"

He laughed. "I think I can't do either. *But*, I can balance a spoon on my nose for a really long time."

I laughed. "Oh yeah? A real show stopper, no doubt."

"Absolutely. It's a can't miss."

We laughed, and I could tell he was thinking the same thing as me. We got along really well.

Tristan yanked open my door and I jumped in surprise. He unexpectedly took my hand and helped me out of the car. Unwarranted tingles raced up my arm. *Dammit*. He didn't release my hand as he leaned in and whispered, "Next time, I'll say no."

A shudder rushed through me as his crisp scent invaded my senses. We'd never been that close before and the intensity was daunting.

He released my hand and returned to the driver's seat.

I balled my hand into a fist at my side, feeling oddly bereft now that he'd released it.

Chris stepped up beside me. "Is that your friend's brother?" he asked, clearly just recognizing Tristan from the party.

I snapped out of the sudden haze I found myself in. "Oh…yeah."

I was such a liar.

Tristan

Kresley's date was a complete tool. I couldn't believe she agreed to go out with a frat guy. That seemed so out of character for her. What the fuck was I saying? I didn't know what was or wasn't out of character for her. I protected her from threats. My job wasn't to analyze who she was and why she did what she did.

I pulled up to the front of her dorm after the bar and threw the car into park. Oh, the kiss goodnight was gonna be fun.

"Well, I had a nice time," Kresley said to the tool, turning to face him in the backseat.

"When are we doing it again?" he asked.

"Text me."

He pulled out his phone as if to text her that moment. She laughed at the lame joke.

"Wait here," he said, before stepping out of his door and rounded the back of the car, opening Kresley's door and helping her out like I had at the bar. Only, he was trying to get a good night kiss while I was putting her in her place. She knew we set protocols in place for a reason. She went rogue by asking me to veer from the plan. And, if Marco found out, I'd have to hear it from him.

I watched out the window as the tool walked her toward the door and leaned in for a kiss. Kresley turned her head so his lips brushed her cheek instead of her lips. *Classic dis.*

Why *hadn't* she kissed him? They seemed to hit it off. She was giving off all the signs that she was into the guy.

He stepped away from her with a smile and said something before turning and disappearing into the darkness.

I expected Kresley to rush into the building, trying to avoid me after she knew we shouldn't have gone anywhere after the restaurant, but she didn't. She stood on the sidewalk as if waiting for me.

I stepped out of the car.

Her face was slanted up at the night sky. "It's too bad we can't always see them," she said.

"See what?" I asked.

"The stars. The lights always ruin the view."

"You know where there are no lights?"

She tore her eyes away from the sky and looked to me.

"The quad."

She raised her eyebrows.

"You should have your boyfriend take you up there sometime," I said, making it clear that I wasn't asking her to go up there with me.

Disappointment flashed across her face but she recovered. "Yeah, right. It would totally kill the mood to have you and Marco lurking in the shadows."

That guy had no game, therefore, there would be no mood-killing going on. "Oh, believe me. We don't watch."

"Like you weren't just watching him try to kiss me."

"Why would I want to see that?"

She shrugged, remaining silent for a long stretch. "Thank you for tonight. I know it takes a lot of planning and effort to secure a place. And, I'm sorry I threw you that open mic night curveball. I just didn't want to be rude and turn him down."

Holy fuck. I stood shocked by her candor.

"You can pick your jaw up off the ground," she said. "I just wanted you to know I appreciate all you do for me."

I wasn't expecting that.

She turned toward the entrance of her dorm and walked toward it.

"I need to go park the car," I said.

She spun back around, her brows drawn in question. "Come with me."

Her eyes widened, caught off guard by my request.

That makes two of us. "Maybe you'll get a better view of the stars," I explained, hating myself for every word coming out of my mouth. I could have easily walked her upstairs then parked the car in the lot.

Her lips tipped up in the corners, and even in the darkness, her blue eyes twinkled. She stepped away from the door and walked over to the car, opening the front passenger door and sliding inside.

I walked back to the driver's side and got in, not bothering to say anything about her sitting in the front seat. I was breaking all the rules anyway.

"It must be boring for you," she said, staring out her window as I drove toward the parking lot.

"What?"

"Having to drive me around, follow me around, sit around."

I shrugged. It had its benefits. There was a lot of downtime, little interaction with people, and always the threat of danger.

"Thanks for sitting outside my door," she said, turning to look at me. "I know you've been there every night."

"You've slept," I said.

"How do you know?"

"Well, you're less of a bitch."

Laughter burst out of her, filling the car with the unfamiliar sound. "I am, aren't I?"

I pulled the car into the parking lot and found a spot. "I was just joking. You don't text to use the bathroom in the middle of the night anymore," I explained as I switched off the engine and turned to look at her. "And, I don't hear footsteps, so I assume you're sleeping."

"After what happened in France," she began, "I had trouble falling asleep. I'd hear his voice taunting me as he pressed his filthy body to mine."

I let her talk, knowing she probably needed to.

"He called me *le fou de fortune*. Fortune's fool. And I'd hear that phrase every time I closed my eyes…My mom started staying in my room. I didn't ask her to, but I think it just made her feel better knowing I was safe. Then, I stopped hearing his voice. I guess I didn't realize until I got here that I needed someone nearby to keep him away."

I'd be lying if I said the knowledge didn't make me regret some of my annoyance with her.

She laughed. "I bet you're thinking, 'Thank God, she didn't ask me to sleep in bed with her'."

"That would definitely be a new one," I agreed, taking that moment to open my door and get out.

Kresley stepped out and looked over the hood of the car at me. "If you're trying to remain stoic to appear tough, I give you permission to smile."

"What?"

She rounded the car until she stood beside me. "I mean, I know I'm funny, so it must be difficult to stop yourself from smiling when you're around me."

"You think you're funny?" I asked.

She smirked. "No, I *know* I'm funny."

A comfortable silence passed between us as we stood there leaned against the side of the car.

"You were right," she said.

I looked to her but her face was slanted toward the sky. I followed her gaze. The dark parking lot allowed for an almost panoramic view of the sky, and all the stars and constellations were visible. It was truly a sight.

"It amazes me that people don't take the time to appreciate the beauty around them. There are so many things we take for granted, and after that night, I swore I wouldn't anymore. I remember being pushed against that wall and knowing he was going to rape me, and all I could do was pray to whoever would listen that if I got a second chance, I'd do things differently. I'd do them right."

I prided myself on being a tough son of a bitch, but I wasn't cold. I was capable of feelings. And the vision of her against that wall—so vulnerable and terrified—fearing for her life, created a pit in my gut. "I'm sure you were a good person before that happened," I said, feeling like I needed to say something after such an honest admission.

"Why do you say that?" she asked.

I shrugged, though I knew her eyes were on the sky. "I'm good at reading people."

"And what—"

My phone rang, interrupting our conversation. I slipped it from my pocket and lifted it to my ear. "Yeah?"

"She with you?" Marco asked, rushed and almost nervous.

"Yeah."

"Where are you?"

"Just about to head back from the parking lot," I explained.

"Get her back to her room. There's been another development and we need to figure out how to proceed."

"Be there in five minutes."

"Stay alert," he warned before hanging up.

Kresley's eyes were trained on mine as I started toward her dorm. "What's wrong?" she asked, following alongside me.

"Nothing."

"Liar."

I picked up the pace as I assessed the surrounding area, unsure what Marco had to tell me once we returned. We'd already received word from our forensics team that there'd been no fingerprints on the package *or* the perfume bottle. There'd also been no way to trace where it had come from. The fuckers who'd sent it went to great lengths, bypassing all the major delivery services, to have that package delivered untraceably. That told us two things. This wasn't over. And the people behind it knew what they were doing.

Marco and I couldn't let our guards down even for a second.

"Tell me what's going on," Kresley said as we neared her dorm. "Should I be worried?"

"You know the threat is always there. But that's why you have security. So, you've got nothing to be worried about."

"This world is so messed up," she said, shaking her head.

"Not telling me something I don't already know."

"When did it become a bad thing for a man to make money from a company he built from the ground up? Why does he now have to worry about people threatening his family to get money they didn't earn?"

"I guess it's the risk of being wealthy," I said.

"Yeah, but I'm not the rich one. I didn't ask for this life."

"Unfortunately, it *is* your life," I said.

We stepped up to the back door of her dorm—the entrance I preferred to use when I was returning from the parking lot. The door unlocked and I pulled it open, checking the empty basement stairwell—only hearing the sound of washing machines running in the laundry room.

As we climbed the steps, I rounded each corner with my eyes open and my hand on my gun at my hip—trying not to give Kresley reason to worry any more than she already was.

"Well, someday, I'm going to live on a small island all by myself," she said as she followed me. "And the only way to get on the island will be by plane or boat. Then I'll always know when someone's coming."

"Sounds like a fairy tale," I said as we stepped out onto our floor.

"Yeah, well, it's my fairy tale," she said as we reached her door.

A small knot formed in my gut. For the first time, I understood. She'd rather be alone on some island so she always knew what threats were coming rather than to live her life the way she was living it. I entered her room, giving it a quick sweep while she waited in the hallway. I stepped back out. "All set." I made to walk to Marco's room.

"Good night, Tristan," Kresley called.

I stopped outside Marco's room and glanced to her. The tool had been right about one thing. She did look beautiful in her red dress. "Night."

Kresley

After slipping into my pajamas, I crawled into bed. Even though it was late, I grabbed my phone and called my mom, needing to know what was going on. Tristan may have been staying tight-lipped, but something was definitely up.

The phone rang twice before she answered. "Kresley?"

"Hi, Mom."

"Sweetie, how are you?" she sounded relieved to hear my voice.

"Good. But I need you to tell me something."

"Okay?" She sounded skeptical.

"Did something else happen that I need to know about?"

"Not that I know of," she said, though something about the way she said it told me she was hiding something. And, since everyone had walked on eggshells with me over the last six months, I had a feeling she didn't want to worry me.

"How'd your date go?" she asked, swiftly changing the subject.

"Chris is nice."

"Just nice?" my mother asked.

"Really nice?"

"But?" My mother was always able to read between the lines.

I sighed. "Why'd you hire Tristan?"

"*Ahhhh*, Tristan," my mother said, like she'd been waiting for me to say something about him. "He's handsome, isn't he?"

"Mom, you know he is."

"I wondered if that would be a problem," she said.

"We actually don't get along most of the time."

"Why not?" she asked.

"It's a long story. But then sometimes…"

"Sometimes what?" she asked.

"Sometimes…he surprises me."

"What does that mean?"

"He's been sitting outside my door so I can sleep."

There was silence on my mom's end.

"Mom?"

"I'm here."

"That's pretty amazing, right?" I said, knowing what a wonderful thing he was doing for me.

"Yes, I'd say it is," she agreed.

I think I needed to hear my mom's reaction to know what I already knew. He couldn't be all bad if he was doing something so nice for me.

We said our goodbyes a few minutes later, right around the time I saw a familiar shadow under my door.

CHAPTER THIRTEEN
Kresley

Marco had been on me like a bee to honey all day Saturday while I studied for an upcoming accounting test in the library. Something was up, but I just didn't know what it was.

"Anything you need to tell me, Marco?" I asked as I struggled with an accounting problem.

"Not that I can think of, ma'am," he replied, much to my annoyance.

The girls stopped by the library later that night delivering me homemade chocolate chip cookies they'd baked in the kitchen in the basement of our dorm. Who knew there was a kitchen in our dorm *or* that they could bake? But the cookies were good. Though, I had to kick them out after a little while because there was no way I was getting studying done with them there.

On Sunday, Marco was waiting outside my door when I stepped out. A tinge of disappointment formed in my stomach that it wasn't Tristan—who I hadn't seen since Friday night. Had he gotten reamed out for taking Chris and me to open mic night?

Marco and I made our way downstairs.

"Anything you need to tell me, Marco?" I asked, trying again.

"Not that I can think of, ma'am," he replied.

We stepped outside. The car was parked at the sidewalk with Tristan in the driver's seat. My disappointment morphed into something else—

something light and eager. Marco pulled open the back door, and I slipped into the backseat. "Thanks, Marco," I said before he shut the door, closing me inside. "Hey, Tristan."

"Hey."

It felt strange seeing him after Friday night. After hearing my mom's reaction to him staying outside my room.

He started the car and a rock song by Savage Beasts blared from the speakers. He quickly lowered it.

"It's fine," I said. "I love that song."

He turned it back up and we drove through the streets of SoCal to the sound of the incomparable—and not to mention gorgeous—Kozart Savage. I'd met lots of celebrities over the years, but none made me as tongue-tied as Kozart had.

"Can you turn that down?" I asked Tristan once the song ended.

He lowered the music.

"Can you tell me why Marco hasn't wanted to leave my side for the last twenty-four hours?"

He shrugged.

"Come on, Tristan. I know you rushed to see him Friday night. You gotta give me something."

He met my eyes in the rearview mirror, and I couldn't stop the goosebumps that scampered up my arms. *Traitorous goosebumps.*

"I know he's not hanging around me because he's hoping I'll be up for a Hallmark marathon."

He remained silent as his eyes moved back to the road.

"Not even a smirk? Come on. That was funny."

What was wrong with him?

A short while later, he pulled down a bumpy dirt road surrounded by tall trees, so unlike the beach-lined streets people thought of when they envisioned Southern California. I stared out the window, anticipation bubbling in my stomach. We came to a stop in front of a one-story structure at the end of the road. The wooden sign staked into the ground out front read: Big Hearts Dog Shelter.

I pushed open the door and stepped out. The overcast sky and impending rain made for a cooler day. Thankfully, I wore my blue hoodie and jeans. I walked to the front door and entered the shelter where I immediately heard dogs barking and yelping.

"You must be Kresley," the old woman behind the counter said. "I'm Doris."

"Nice to meet you. I'm so excited to be here," I said before my eyes were drawn to all the cages and the eager dogs of all sizes inside them.

"I'm excited to have you. The dogs need exercise."

I smiled. "Just tell me what I need to do and I'll get started."

She walked me through the room of cages that lined both walls. Every dog jumped on the cage door, wagging their tails and barking as we walked by, trying to get our attention.

"Hey there," I said to a little pug. "Hi you," I greeted a long-haired dachshund. "Aren't you a cutie pie," I said, petting a German shepherd's nose.

Doris pointed out the leashes hanging by each dog's cage, the waste bags I'd need to use to keep the walking path clean, and a variety of dog treats to use as praise. She gave me my pick of dogs to start with, telling me they each needed a good fifteen-minute walk. I could take three small dogs at once, but only one large one.

I gathered the three small dogs I chose to walk first, leashed them, then headed out toward the front door.

"Just stay on the path, sweetie," Doris called as I opened the door and stepped outside.

Tristan leaned against the SUV staring down at his phone. Who was he texting? A girlfriend? His mother? Whoever it was, he didn't even look up as the dogs led me eagerly to the path. I heard Tristan's footsteps trailing behind me as I took the wooded path. Within no time, the dogs pulled me to the side, all lifting their legs on various trees or bushes.

"We have security working at the office too," Tristan finally said, breaking his long stretch of silence.

I twisted to look at him standing beside me. "What?"

"You asked what I knew. And I'm telling you we have guys at the office who work cybersecurity who monitor the internet and dark web. They're privy to all the seedy goings-on that people like you never want to know about."

"And?" I prompted.

"And…there's been money exchanged to get to you."

I sucked in a sharp breath.

"No one wants you to know," he said. "But it's your life we're talking about. You need to know what's happening so you can be prepared."

I nodded, totally *un*prepared for that information. I knew it was always a possibility, but hearing that something was set in motion, and we didn't know when or where it could occur, sent a shiver skimming down my spine.

"Are you scared?" he asked.

"Yes."

"But you know that's why Marco and I are here. To make sure nothing happens to you."

I nodded. "I know."

"Should I have told you?" he asked.

"Probably not. But I'm glad you did." Tears glazed my eyes and there wasn't a thing I could do to stop them from falling.

He cursed under his breath.

I shook my head, wiping my eyes with the backs of my hands, leashes and all. "No. I need to know. I'm not a child. I have to know these things."

He moved toward me, stopping when the toes of our shoes nearly touched. I tipped back my head to meet his gaze. For the first time, I saw concern in his eyes. "I will protect you, Kresley. You have my word."

I closed my eyes, wanting to believe that more than I ever wanted to believe anything in my life.

CHAPTER FOURTEEN
Tristan

I expected Kresley to want to leave the dog shelter after I'd told her what everyone else had been too nervous to, but she surprised me, finishing the first walk and heading back to retrieve more dogs. I wondered if it was a defense mechanism for her to occupy herself with mundane things to not have to deal with reality. But if that's what she was doing, it was working.

"Do you volunteer at home, too?" I asked her as the three new dogs pulled her to the same path we'd just walked on.

"Yeah. My parents always instilled in me that it was important to give back. And they were right."

"Do you always walk dogs?" I asked, following alongside her.

She laughed. "No. I usually visit hospitals and help feed the homeless. I just thought animals were safer this time around."

She had a point. People were unpredictable. Animals you could rely on to be loyal as long as you fed them and walked them.

"It's why I'm majoring in hospitality to be an event planner. I want to assist nonprofit organizations with their fundraising events. If they have me, they can solely focus on grant writing, securing investors, and looking for support, while I take care of the event and all that entails."

People *were* unpredictable. I expected Kresley's motives for becoming an event planner to be superficial. Like, making the world better one wedding or fashion show at a time. But I was starting to see Kresley was a lot more real than I initially expected. And I wasn't sure what to do with that knowledge.

"Why'd you open Elite Security?" she asked.

"How'd you know it's mine?"

"I did some research. I obviously needed to know who was protecting me. So, why security?" she persisted.

"I wanted to protect people who couldn't protect themselves."

"Like me?" She held my gaze as if trying to read my expression.

I shrugged.

"Has anyone under your protection ever been shot?" she asked.

My eyes shifted away, and I felt anger flaring up inside me. "If you're worried that I can't properly protect you—"

"I didn't say that," she cut me off. "It was just a question."

"Then yes. Two people under my protection were shot." I pressed my lips together, cursing myself for admitting that to her. That was *my* business. Not hers.

She was quiet for a long time, and I wondered what my honesty elicited in her. Fear? Disgust? Anger? "Let's get something straight," she said, her voice taking on an I-can-say-what-I-want-because-I'm-a-rich-girl tone. "Unless I say something outright, don't assume what I *might* say. Let me say it first."

My hand tightened into a fist at my side, pissed she was trying to put me in my place after I'd been honest with her numerous times.

"Maybe that's where our problems stem from," she continued. "You think you know me, but you don't."

Ah, but I do. On the surface, despite nearly being raped and kidnapped, she was strong and confident—making friends easily and opting to volunteer on her Sundays. But underneath the surface, what people didn't know, what they couldn't know because she was too proud to admit it, was that demons haunted her dreams keeping her awake at night.

Kresley

Rain began to drop from the sky as I took the old German shepherd for the final walk of the day. Knowing thunderstorms were on the way, I tried to hurry the slow dog along, giving him a gentle tug. "Come on, buddy. It's starting to rain."

The dog rebelled, sitting down and staring up at me.

Tristan snickered nearby.

I gave the dog another light tug. Still, he wouldn't budge. Just then, the sky opened up and rain poured down through the trees. I lifted my face to the heavens and uncontrollable laughter tumbled out of me. How was I even able to laugh after what Tristan had told me? But there I stood laughing with rain soaking every inch of me.

"What's so funny?" Tristan asked.

I kept my eyes closed as I breathed in the rain-filled forest air. "I'm just appreciating the things around me."

"Come on," he called over the pitter-patter of the hard rain on the trees and ground.

I finally looked to him

Tristan was just as drenched as me. His hair hung over his forehead and raindrops dangled from his long eyelashes making him look so much younger than he usually did. He took the leash from my hand, giving the dog a slight tug.

Instantly, the dog stood.

"Seriously?" I shook my head then took off running through the woods, my feet splashing in muddy puddles as I ran.

I could hear Tristan's footsteps, as well as the dog's, slapping the mud behind me.

Back at the shelter, I threw open the door and rushed inside. Tristan was only a few steps behind me. We dripped rain all over the floor.

"Oh, no. You got caught in the downpour!" Doris said as the German shepherd shook the rain off his fur, sending water flying everywhere.

I continued to laugh as I dried him off and got him back into his cage. "See you next time, you stubborn old dog," I whispered to him.

CHAPTER FIFTEEN
Kresley

When we returned to the SUV, I slid into the front seat, loving the fact that Tristan didn't tell me to get in the back. He dragged his fingers through his wet hair as I unzipped my drenched hoodie and tossed it onto the floor in the backseat. He started the engine and cranked the heat.

We were quiet as we drove back toward campus. I wondered if Tristan had resorted back to his silent self from earlier *or* if he was wishing he hadn't told me what he'd told me—about the money being exchanged *and* the two people shot under his watch. "Are you hungry? I'm hungry," I said, suddenly not in a rush to get back to the dorm.

Tristan turned to look at me. "What are you in the mood for?"

"Ice cream."

"It's lunchtime."

"Best kind of lunch," I assured him.

His lips twitched. "Fine. But we're only hitting the drive-up."

I smiled. "Perfect."

We took a detour to find an ice cream shop with a drive-up window. I ordered a chocolate cone and Tristan got a strawberry shake. It almost felt normal. Like we were just two college kids driving around SoCal eating ice cream for lunch. But that couldn't have been further from the truth. I was a rich man's daughter at risk of being used as a pawn in a dangerous game, and he was my bodyguard who couldn't decide how he felt about me.

He glanced at me, catching me staring. "You're not so bad when you're eating ice cream," he said.

"Oh, yeah? Why's that?" I asked, fishing for anything from him that could help me get to know him better.

"It stops you from talking so damn much."

My mouth fell open. "That is *not* the way you talk to your employer."

"Oh, I'd never speak to your dad that way," he assured me before sipping more of his shake.

"You're a real jerk," I said.

"Never said I wasn't."

I looked over at him as he continued drinking his milkshake with his eyes on the road. He was such a good-looking guy. I just wished he'd smile because I bet he had a great smile.

We returned to the dorm a little while later. Tristan waited outside the bathroom while I showered, needing to warm my chilled bones. Then, I settled in for the night. I had a bunch of homework to do, but I found it impossible to concentrate.

Around midnight, I saw Tristan's shadow beneath my door. I breathed a sigh of relief, then crawled under my comforter and closed my eyes, listening to the rain that hadn't let up all day. I lay there for a long time, waiting for sleep to come like it normally did once he was there, but it never came. I tossed and turned while the rain pelted my window, no longer a soothing sound.

I started thinking about what Tristan had told me. Someone had actually been paid money to get to me. Then, my mind drifted to what happened in France, and I couldn't shake the visions. The feel of the Frenchman pressed against me. The mocking sound of his voice. *Le fou de fortune.*

Lightning flickered, momentarily lighting up my room.

I closed my eyes, trying to shake the sight of Andre's face that suddenly appeared in my mind's eyes. The pain. The fear. The regret. The blood.

I opened my eyes only to be startled by the dark shadows dancing across my walls.

Thunder boomed, shaking the floor beneath my bed. I practically jumped out of my skin.

Enough!

I kicked off my comforter and slipped out of bed. I began to pace the floor. Back and forth. Side to side. Around in a circle.

Repeat.

"Get in bed," Tristan whispered through the door.

Of course he knew I was up.

I moved to the door, pressing my ear to the hard surface, needing to hear his voice more than ever.

"I'm right here," he assured me.

I reached down and unlocked the door. I grasped the knob, knowing better than to contemplate my next move. Because if I did, I'd be pacing the floor all night. I slowly twisted the knob and cracked open the door.

Tristan felt me open the door from his spot on the floor. He sat forward and turned to look up at me through the crack. "What are you doing?"

"Will you come inside?"

His brows shot up. "What?"

"I'm having trouble sleeping."

He cocked his head, indecision heavy in his eyes.

"Just for a little bit," I assured him. "I need to see if it'll work."

"Dammit," he cursed, his eyes dodging mine. "I never should've told you."

"Of course you should've. You're the only one who's been honest with me."

He closed his eyes, seemingly pained by what I was asking him to do. After what felt like an eternity, his eyes opened and he pushed himself to his feet. His basketball shorts hung low on his hips and his T-shirt clung to his muscles. He readjusted what I knew to be his gun holster underneath as he stepped forward. Relief swept over me as I moved back and he stepped inside, closing the door behind him. "Get in bed."

Under any other circumstance, I would've been turned on by a man telling me to get into bed; however, his was an order so I could sleep—and he could get out of my room as quickly as possible. I moved to my bed and slipped under the comforter, turning onto my side as he pulled the chair out from my desk and sat in it. "Thank you, Tristan."

"Sleep," he ordered, crossing his arms and looking surly.

"I hope so." I closed my eyes and pushed the new threat, the Frenchman, and Andre from my mind, reminding myself that Tristan was right there and he wouldn't let anything happen to me.

Tristan

What the fuck was I doing? I was breaking protocols on so many levels. Not to mention, if Marco caught me in her room, he'd be ripping me a new one for the foreseeable future.

But I couldn't deny her this.

I couldn't deny her this because *I* was to blame.

I'd been the one to open my damn mouth and tell her the shit that had been going on behind her back. I'd been the one to put the thoughts in her head that likely kept her from sleeping. But I'd never been one to shy away from the truth. Like what I had to say or not, it wouldn't stop me from saying it.

And as much as it sucked that she couldn't sleep, I wouldn't take back telling her what I knew—what *everyone* but her knew. She deserved the truth. She deserved to know some fucked up people out there were dead set on getting her. And, despite the fact that we didn't know who those fuckers were, or where or when they might strike, it would still be a cold day in hell before I let anyone get to her.

A small sigh escaped Kresley, pulling my attention to her. She'd fallen asleep, but could I slip out without waking her? Or, should I wait to be sure she didn't wake up?

Fuck me.

CHAPTER SIXTEEN
Kresley

I heard the *click* of my door closing the following morning. I didn't need to look to know it was Tristan. I also didn't need to question if his presence had worked since I slept soundly all night. Unfortunately, I was left to wonder if I'd be able to sleep without him in my room moving forward.

I stayed in bed for a little longer before texting Marco for a shower. I wondered if he checked my camera feed last night and saw Tristan in my room. And, if he had, would he say anything about it. But when he picked me up for my shower, and then again to walk me to class, he didn't say anything. Like, not a word.

I glanced over at him by my side, but his eyes were on everything but me as we made our way up the path toward my first class. Was he mad? Was he worried?

"I know," I said.

His eyes cut to mine, narrowing.

"I know there was money exchanged."

"Son of a *bitch*," he said through clenched teeth.

"Don't get mad at Tristan. I need to know this stuff, Marco. I need to know what I'm up against."

"It's our job to be your eyes and ears."

"If I was your wife, would you tell me?"

He said nothing.

"Of course you would because you'd want me to be prepared."

He remained quiet, likely considering the validity of what I'd said.

We arrived to my class and I disappeared inside, losing myself in communications before finding my seat in accounting after that for my big test.

"So, I showed up at Sigma Chi and both Reggie and Simon were there," a girl somewhere behind me told her friend.

"No way."

"Yeah. They both found out and neither was too happy."

Her friend laughed. "It was bound to happen eventually.

A tinge of jealousy swarmed in my stomach, wishing just once that I could be a normal college girl with normal college girl drama.

"Hey," Jeff said, slipping into the seat beside me, his dreadlocks pulled back into a ponytail at his neck.

"Hey," I said, snapping out of the pity party I'd been throwing myself.

"Have a good weekend?"

If you consider finding out someone's coming after me, then yeah, totally. "It was okay."

"Okay?" he questioned. "You mean you weren't triple booked for dates all weekend?"

"Triple booked?"

"Yeah. You're telling me none of these guys has scooped you up yet?" Jeff said.

"There may be a few possibilities," I joked.

"A few? Girl, you've been here for two weeks and you only have a few?"

I laughed. "Yeah, I'm totally failing at my game."

"I'd say." He laughed, and for a moment, I actually did feel like a normal college girl. I just wished that feeling would last.

* * *

"So, have you heard from Chris since you gave him the cheek?" Elodie asked over dinner.

"Don't you have some freshman who requires your help back at the dorm?" I asked before taking a bite of my veggie burger.

Alice laughed and looked to Elodie. "They ate Italian food. He must've had garlic breath. Gross."

Elodie raised a brow. "Did he?"

I shrugged, noncommittal.

"Why are you grilling her?" Alice asked, popping an onion ring into her mouth. "That's usually my thing."

"I want her to admit what we all know," Elodie said.

I cocked my head. "What do we all know?"

Elodie glanced around the room, ready to say something she didn't want anyone—including Marco who stood against a nearby wall—to hear. "That you want your bodyguard."

My eyes widened.

Elodie pushed her glasses up her nose. "Tell me I'm wrong."

"You're wrong," I assured her.

She looked unconvinced. "I've seen him outside your room."

"So?"

"So, have you ever heard of a movie star's bodyguard sitting on the floor outside her room?"

"I'm not a movie star," I countered.

"Well, if we're not getting any action—"

"Speak for yourself," Alice cut Elodie off.

Elodie rolled her eyes. "If *I'm* not getting any action, someone needs to."

"What my friend is trying to say," Alice interrupted. "Is that since you have a sexy as hell man sitting right outside your door…"

I gnawed on my bottom lip as my eyes wandered from hers, knowing his post *outside* my room may have changed to *inside* my room.

Elodie pointed across the table at me, accusingly. "What aren't you telling us?"

"Nothing."

"Tell us," Alice said, leaning closer and clearly jumping on the grilling bandwagon. *Traitor.*

"He may have sat *in* my room last night."

They both threw back their heads and groaned dramatically.

"What the hell?" Elodie whined.

"Girl, you are the luckiest person I've ever met," Alice said.

I used to feel like one of the luckiest girls in the world. My dad always made sure to make me feel that way. But after France, I felt like fate was plotting against me. Hell, the Frenchman all but assured me that it was.

"He definitely wants you," Elodie said.

"He's just making sure I'm safe."

Alice popped another onion ring into her mouth. "Safe my ass."

* * *

I finished my homework around eleven then changed into my pajamas and climbed into bed. I lay on my side facing the door, waiting for Tristan's shadow to appear. Would I need to ask him to come in? Would he wait to see if I paced the floor? Would he just come in?

My conversation with the girls over dinner played through my mind. Had they been right about what I may or may not have been feeling? My life was such a mess and threatening to only get worse. Could I really be having feelings for my bodyguard? Or was I just feeling appreciative that he was looking out for me and being honest about the threats against me when no one else was?

There was a light tap on my door after midnight. I crawled out of bed and padded over to the door, pressing my ear to it.

"Kresley?" Tristan whispered.

Goosebumps erupted on my skin. *Dammit.* I opened my door.

Tristan stood there in shorts and a T-shirt but made no move to enter my room.

"Are you coming in?" I asked.

He hesitated. "Is that what you need?"

I stared into his eyes for a long time. Did he want to come in? Was he only doing what he thought I needed? "I'm not sure. But I kind of think so."

He stepped forward and I stepped back into my room.

My heart drummed faster. A rush of emotions, and dare I say desire, flooded me. This feeling I was having—this pull—was not what I felt for Chris. This was something else. Something I was having more and more difficulty shutting off even though I needed to.

Tristan moved into my room and closed the door. "Get into bed."

"Do you say that to all the girls?"

His glare told me he was in no mood for jokes.

"Sorry," I mumbled as I climbed underneath my comforter and turned onto my side to face him.

He sat in the desk chair beside my bed. He leaned forward with his elbows resting on his thighs and his hands wringing in front of him.

"You okay?" I asked.

"Fine."

"You don't look fine."

"And you don't look like you're asleep. Go to sleep."

I lay there with my eyes open, watching him contemplating something for a long time.

His eyes finally cut to mine. "You told Marco what I told you."

"Is that a problem?" I asked.

He shrugged.

"Are you mad?"

"Why aren't you sleeping?" he clipped.

"You do realize you've got split personalities, right?"

He glared at me.

"There's nice Tristan. Then bossy Tristan. And, my least favorite, mean Tristan."

"Well, all three Tristan's can take their ass across the hall and leave you alone." He made to stand.

"And then there's stubborn Tristan. And stubborn Tristan can sit his ass down."

He scoffed.

"I haven't seen a ring on your finger," I said. "Does that mean no woman has been able to put up with all four Tristans?"

"I'm only twenty-five."

"People get married at all ages."

"If they're crazy," he countered.

I rolled my eyes.

"Why aren't you sleeping?" he asked, his frustration evident in his tone.

"I'm just curious about you. Is there something wrong with that? We spend time together. I just want to know more about you."

He closed his eyes and dragged in a long breath.

Was I pissing him off? Was he regretting his decision to come into my room?

When he opened his eyes, there was a glimmer of resignation there. Then he sighed. "What do you want to know?"

Shit. I hadn't considered he'd offer that up to me on a silver platter. Did I ask if he had a girlfriend? Did I ask where he grew up? Did I ask if he planned to work as a bodyguard forever? "Do you bowl?" I blurted.

His brows arched, seemingly just as surprised by my question as I was. "Do I bowl?"

"It's a perfectly legitimate question."

He chuckled. "I don't know. If I have to."

"Good to know." I turned over in bed and closed my eyes.

Maybe I hadn't learned anything of any real value, but I had made Tristan Stone laugh. And, I really liked knowing I had.

***

"No...stop...please...no..."

My eyes popped open, Tristan's words yanking me from a sound sleep.

His head was down as he sat in my chair, asleep but speaking. "Please...don't..."

I froze, not sure what I should do. He was having a nightmare. A terrible nightmare. The pained expression on his face and the desperation in his words shook me to the core. I'd rarely seen his tough exterior falter, so to see this vulnerable side of him rendered me incapable of clear thoughts. I climbed out of bed and crept over to him, careful not to scare him. I kneeled in front of him and placed my hands gently on his thighs. "Tristan?" I whispered.

His eyes sprang open, and he clutched his shirt where his gun lay underneath.

"No! You're okay. Everything's okay. You were dreaming," I assured him with my heart racing in my chest.

As if coming out of a trance, he blinked multiple times.

"You were just dreaming," I assured him. *Holy hell, he could've shot me.*

"Fuck," he growled as he pushed himself to his feet.

The sudden movement sent me reeling back and I landed on my butt.

He didn't move to help me up. Instead, he ran his hands through his hair and started pacing the floor. "How long was I asleep?"

I pushed myself to my feet and grabbed for my phone on the desk. "A few hours. It's three."

"*Fuck.*"

"I think you were having a nightmare," I said as I sat on my bed, hoping he'd tell me what he'd been dreaming about.

He avoided my gaze and walked to the door. "I'm gonna sit out there." He twisted the doorknob.

"Tristan?"

He stopped before opening the door but didn't turn around.

"I'm here if you need me."

He shook his head, mumbling something I couldn't hear as he yanked open the door and walked out.

Thunder outside coincided with the ominous click of the door closing me alone inside my room.

I stared at the door glimpsing Tristan's shadow beneath it. At least he hadn't abandoned me completely.

I understood his embarrassment. He was a big bad bodyguard. He couldn't have nightmares. He couldn't show weakness. But didn't he realize that only made him more human in my eyes? We all had our demons. It didn't define us.

And, though I'd never push him on the issue since it clearly unnerved him, I was curious to know what plagued his dreams. Because most people didn't react the way he did if it was just a rare nightmare. His reaction told me it had happened before, and he hated that I witnessed it.

What secrets was Tristan hiding?

And, what didn't he want me to know?

CHAPTER SEVENTEEN
Kresley

Marco walked me back to the dorm after my last class the next day. I had a ton of work to do, but I was exhausted since I didn't sleep after Tristan left my room the previous night.

I unpacked my backpack and was about to dive into planning a mock event for my special events class when there was a soft tapping on my door.

"Kresley?" Tristan asked.

I moved to the door, stopping before opening it. "Yeah?"

"Can I talk to you?"

I stilled. Was something wrong? Did he want to explain what happened the previous night? I opened the door, unable to stop myself from drinking in his dark jeans, navy short-sleeve shirt, and ballcap pulled low on his head. He looked like a college guy ready to head out to class. "What's up?"

"I was…" he began, his eyes avoiding mine. "I'd like to take you somewhere."

My head hitched back, not expecting that. "Where?"

He met my eyes but shook his head as if he wanted to tell me but he couldn't.

"My security team would tell me to beware of people acting strange and not telling me where they wanted to take me," I said.

"If I tell you, you may not want to go. And I really want you to come with me."

My brows shot up, curious where he wanted to take me. "Does Marco know you're here?"

He shook his head.

"Would Marco be okay with us going somewhere?" I asked.

"Probably not."

Something about him wanting to take me somewhere and Marco not being happy about it if he knew intrigued me. *Damn you, Tristan.* "Okay. But you need to let Marco know I'm with you so he doesn't flip out."

"I'll text him once we're in the car."

"We're driving somewhere?"

He nodded.

I looked down at my cutoffs and long-sleeve T-shirt. "Is what I'm wearing appropriate?"

His eyes dragged slowly over my body causing a shiver to dance across my skin. "Yeah." His eyes shot away, clearly not wanting to be inappropriate.

I grabbed my money and ID from my backpack and tucked them into my back pocket. "All set…I think."

The car was parked at the sidewalk when we stepped outside. I opened the front door and hopped in. Tristan circled the car and slipped into the driver's seat. I turned to look at him as he started the car.

He noticed me looking at him. "What?"

"Just waiting for you to text Marco. I need someone to know where I am."

"What are you accusing me of?"

I shrugged. "One can never be too careful."

"I'm your security, for God's sake."

"Yeah, but when have you ever wanted to take me anywhere?"

He rolled his eyes, not bothering with a response. He pulled away and started driving.

"In case you didn't realize, you still haven't texted Marco," I said after a few minutes of silence.

He growled. "Are you always this—"

"Amazing?" I asked.

"No."

"Wonderful?"

"Nope."

"Fantastic?"

He huffed, seemingly overwhelmed by my awesomeness.

We drove for another few minutes, crossing into the next town. It was filled with quaint little shops and cafés on both sides of the street. Shoppers walked down the sidewalks with bags of new purchases. "It's cute around here."

"I thought you were more of a beach girl," he said.

I looked at him. "Why?"

"The pictures in your room," he explained. "They're all beaches."

"I told you. I want to live on a private island one day. Those pictures remind me that anything's possible."

He switched on his blinker and pulled into a parking lot. The lot was bigger than it appeared, wrapping around the back of a building off a side street—away from the shops and restaurants that made the town so charming.

There were no signs on the two-story brick building, but there was a single metal door on the ground floor. "What is this place?"

"You'll see." He cut the engine and composed a text, holding up his phone once he'd sent it off. "I texted Marco. Happy?"

"Very."

He opened his door and stepped out.

I followed his lead, meeting him at the back of the SUV where he pulled a black bag out of the rear door. "If I knew we were picnicking, I would have made little sandwiches."

"Do you always need to be such a smartass?"

"Do you always need to be so surly? You're twenty-five. Not elderly."

He slammed the back of the SUV and walked toward the metal door of the building.

I followed him, hating how his personality changed from one minute to the next. I glanced around for signs as we stopped at the door. Tristan pounded twice with the side of his fist, then we waited.

"Is it worth mentioning that I'm getting a little freaked out right now?"

"You're with *me*. You've got nothing to worry about," he assured me.

The door squeaked open, and a bald man with a huge gray beard wearing a wife-beater opened the door. Tristan flashed him some type of identification and the guy motioned us in with the jerk of his head.

The man disappeared as I followed Tristan down a dim hallway. The sound of gunshots caused me to stop in my tracks. "What is this place?"

"I'm gonna teach you how to protect yourself."

I stared across the space between us, unsure if I was terrified or relieved.

"It's good for you to know how to handle a gun. Most civilians—especially women—don't." He turned and continued walking.

I followed him to a room at the end of the hallway. It was set up for target practice, but instead of silhouette pictures hanging in the distance like in the movies, this room had different real-life objects scattered around—all filled with bullet holes: mannequins, rawhide sacks, logs, cans, fences, mounds of dirt, a door with the glass missing.

"Have you ever fired a gun before?" he asked me.

I shook my head, too terrified to ever even hold a gun.

"Does your father own a gun?"

I shrugged. "We have security. Why would he need one?"

Tristan placed his bag down on a shelf and unzipped it, pulling out protective glasses. He slipped on a pair and handed me the other. "Put these on."

I did, hoping the small precaution would ease my anxiety over shooting a gun. It didn't.

Tristan reached back in the bag and pulled out a small black gun. I could see bigger guns inside the bag and hoped to God he didn't think I was going to be shooting any of those. He held the grip of the small gun out to me. "Here," he said, urging it toward me.

I shook my head. "I'm scared."

"I'd be worried if you weren't," he said, placing the gun sideways in his open palm and holding it out to me. "This is yours. It's been registered in your name. Pick it up by the grip and then hold it however you feel comfortable. Just keep your finger off the trigger and point it away from me."

"You think?"

He chuckled, and I appreciated him being amused because my heart sped exponentially as I took the gun and held it, making sure to point it away from us. It was lighter than I expected.

"It's not loaded," he said, reading my mind. "We're gonna practice aiming it without bullets first."

I released a breath. "Great idea."

He pulled another gun from his bag and showed me how to hold it away from my body and without my finger on the trigger.

I mimicked his move.

"Stand with your feet shoulder-width apart," he said.

I did as told.

"Your right hand is your dominant hand, so have your right foot slightly back."

I slipped my right foot back a few inches.

He bent his legs a little. "Knees are slightly bent."

I bent my legs slightly.

"Bend over your waist a tiny bit." He did it to show me.

I followed his lead, feeling a little uncomfortable.

"You'll lose balance with the recoil if you're upright and that won't work."

I nodded, trying to take it all in.

"Let's talk about your eyes."

"I've been told they're pretty," I said, trying to lighten the serious mood.

"Smartass."

I smiled, though it quickly faded.

"I want you to do everything in your power to keep both eyes open when you shoot. People tend to close their eyes or only keep one eye open, but I want you to work hard to keep both eyes open so you're not cutting off half or all of your vision. You can squint if that's easier."

"Both eyes open. Squint. Got it."

"Okay, now I need you to find a spot and aim at it. Start with a larger target that's about seven yards away, like that mannequin," he said pointing at the bullet-riddled mannequin.

I lifted the gun in one hand.

"Be sure your finger is not on the trigger yet."

I nodded.

"Now, use your left hand to grab the grip almost over your right hand so you're giving yourself complete support."

I did what he said and could feel the added support of two hands.

"Now, keep your arms steady and find your target with both eyes. Do you see it?"

I nodded.

"Move your finger to the trigger."

"Now?"

"Yes."

"You sure?"

"You can do it," he assured me, his tone becoming comforting and kind.

The steel of the gun was cold and the idea that I was about to shoot it was terrifying. "Like this?" I asked as I slipped my finger onto the trigger.

"Perfect. Now, keep your eyes open and on your target."

I nodded.

"Now, pull the trigger."

I locked eyes on the bare chest of the mannequin and squeezed the trigger. The gun clicked. I looked to Tristan with the gun still aimed at the mannequin. "Was that good?"

"I'd say you hit his heart."

"Liar."

He chuckled again, and the sound brought a lightness to my chest that the otherwise grim setting had dulled. "Let's try a few more targets, then I'll load the gun."

I swallowed around the lump that shot to my throat.

He pointed across the way. "Try that sack on the ground."

* * *

As we drove through town on our way back to campus, my body buzzed with an unfamiliar feeling. I'd shot a gun. And the power I felt behind that weapon, knowing I could protect myself if I needed to, was a true adrenaline rush—both gratifying and terrifying all wrapped up in one. "Why'd you really take me there today?" I asked Tristan.

He looked at me. "You need to be able to protect yourself."

"No, I'm serious, Tristan. Why?"

"What happened to your bodyguard in France?" he asked.

I flinched at the mention of Andre, his question sucking the air right out of the car.

"Those men were able to get past him to get to you. Shit happens. I'm no superhero, Kresley. If I get shot, there's a chance they could get to you."

"Are you trying to make me feel better or scare the hell out me?"

"I just want you to be prepared for anything." He looked at me and then to the road. "I'm sure growing up you always thought nothing would happen to you. Like the security your parents required for you was unnecessary. But then it wasn't."

I said nothing because he hit the nail on the head. As a teenager, I'd been annoyed by my security, especially since a lot of my friends could come and go as they pleased without having to clear it with anyone.

"And I bet you thought nothing would happen to your bodyguard. But then it did. You need to be prepared." He leveled me with his eyes. "And now you are."

I turned to the window and stared out, trying to stop my racing heart from bouncing around in my chest. He'd brought up France *and* Andre. Two things I tried to never think about. Look where it got me the other night. As soon as I opened up to Tristan about the Frenchman taunting me, images of that horrific night filled my nightmares.

"I'm sorry if this is hard for you to hear," he continued.

I shook my head before glancing back to him. "Thanks for taking me. It means a lot."

"Let's just hope you never need to use your new skills."

"You mean my new, super-secret, assassin skills?" I said.

He chuckled, the deep sound filling the SUV and easing the tension I'd been feeling since we'd been talking about France. "Let's not get crazy now."

"Hey, you're the one who gave me a gun."

"To keep under your bed," he stressed. "Promise me you'll never take it out unless necessary."

"You don't have to worry. Having that thing in my hand terrifies me. I won't be playing with it any time soon."

"Good."

We drove for a little while before I asked, "Did you think I did a good job. You know, for my first time?"

"Yeah. I'd possibly consider having you as my bodyguard in like ten years if you keep up the good work."

I absorbed the details of his face and the way his eyes softened at the edges. "Was that a joke? Because I think that was a joke."

He shrugged.

"Tristan Stone is officially a comedian. Not a very good one. But in maybe ten years or so, he just might bring down the house."

Tristan

I wouldn't lie and say Kresley didn't make me laugh. Okay, maybe I'd lie to *her* about it. But, truthfully, she had a great personality for someone who should've been in daily counseling or on heavy meds for what she'd endured. And, being around her had its benefits. She smelled great. Had a killer body. And she wasn't terrible to look at.

Working security definitely hardened a person. You always expected the worst from people, waiting for the next scumbag to come out of the woodwork to pose a threat for your client. So, having a little of Kresley's femininity rub off on me, making me feel warm in all the right places when most of my life had been dark, hadn't necessarily been a bad thing.

And did I mention what a complete badass she'd been shooting the gun? She'd gotten bolder as our training session went on, firing at will with confidence in her abilities. And I knew, if she ever needed to handle a gun again, she'd feel more comfortable—at least more comfortable than she'd been when we arrived at the gun range. But I wasn't delusional enough to think that had cured her of her bad dreams. I knew once we were back at the dorm, she'd be scared to close her eyes. It was such a paradox. One I certainly wasn't able to explain. But one I knew all too well.

Silence descended upon the car. I was used to her grilling me to get me talking. But she had gotten quiet. And that freaked me the hell out. Was she gearing up to ask me about my nightmare? Because that was not a conversation I planned to have with her. I wasn't the type of guy to open myself up to people—especially clients. And while I knew Kresley would've appreciated it if I did—seeing as though she was so forthcoming with what she'd been through, it was as if I wasn't in control of my mouth when I was around her. I just couldn't *not* push her buttons. Just like she couldn't *not* push mine. It's what our entire relationship had been based on. And I didn't know how to stop.

CHAPTER EIGHTEEN
Tristan

"She wants to do what?" I asked Marco as we stood outside of Kresley's class the next day.

"She wants us to go bowling with her and her two friends," he repeated.

"She's lost her damn mind. Does she not understand our job is to protect her? How the hell can we protect her while we're fucking bowling?"

He shrugged. "It's her birthday."

"Her birthday?" How did I not know that?

He nodded. "I think she's just looking for a little normalcy. She suffered a traumatic experience. And now she's away from home again in a new place with threats still out there. I think she's just trying to create a sense of security with a safe group of people."

I didn't say anything because I understood. After I'd lost my parents, I only had my grandfather. I would've given anything to have more people to surround me— and distract me from the nightmares plaguing my mind.

"She trusts us," Marco continued. "Therefore, she wants to keep us close. Our job makes it so we're always on the outskirts but never quite in the mix. I think she needs us in the mix."

"But that's not part of the job description."

"Neither is sitting inside her room." He cocked his head. "Or taking her for target practice."

I'd been waiting for him to broach the subject, but now that he had, I had no good response. Taking her to the shooting range had been a spur of the moment decision. Because, one, I wanted to distract her from what happened in her room when I fell asleep. That *never* should have happened given I was on duty. And, two, she needed to know how to protect herself. The threat against her was real. And, I wasn't going to treat it like it wasn't.

Kresley

"This is so *Grease 2*," Alice said as Marco opened the back door when we arrived at the bowling alley.

"I love that movie," I said as she scooted out of the backseat. "It's totally underrated."

"Agreed," Alice said.

"This is gonna be so much fun!" Elodie said as she followed Alice out.

Tristan opened my door.

I stepped out with my birthday tiara and sash on and lifted my brows. "Excited?"

He rolled his eyes but I just smiled, because he and Marco were wearing jeans and dark shirts, looking more like willing partygoers than bodyguards forced to have fun with me. And, even if they hated the idea of being there, they were playing along.

As soon as we entered the bowling alley, the *crack* of pins being knocked down filled the air. Chatter from groups spread out on various lanes filled me with excitement. *This was going to be so much fun!*

Two guys in dark security gear approached Marco and Tristan, speaking with their voices low. No wonder they agreed to go bowling. They'd called in backup.

The alternate security guards, who looked to be about Tristan's age, led us to our lane. They were both stocky with buzz cuts.

Our multi-colored shoes awaited us at our lane, so we found our sizes and slipped into them. Alice took off for the nearby bar, passing our new bodyguards with her signature curtsy. She returned before we'd even finished picking out our bowling balls with a pitcher of beer for us to share. Marco and Tristan shook their heads. Even though I'd given them the night off—kind of—they still felt as though they were on duty.

Alice filled three plastic cups. She grabbed her cup and lifted it. Elodie and I followed her lead. "May twenty-two be your best year yet! Happy Birthday!"

My cheeks heated, hating the attention, but I tapped my glass to theirs nonetheless with a smile on my face— so lucky to have found two girls who'd taken me in and made me one of their own.

I downed half my cup then sat on the outdated white and brown plastic bench as Elodie got up to bowl.

Marco and Tristan stood off to the side with their bowling shoes on and arms crossed.

"You two need to loosen up," I said. "You're lucky I didn't make you go clubbing with us."

"That's next," Alice declared with her cup raised in the air.

We took turns bowling, but it was no surprise that Marco and Tristan were kicking our asses. But I didn't care. I sat back and watched everyone, taking it all in. It seemed so normal. So unlike my life. Elodie and Alice were having so much fun even though most of their balls landed in the gutter. Their laughter was infectious and I had no choice but to join in. This night was about so much more than bowling for me—or my birthday for that matter. This was about finding the people I felt comfortable and safe with. It was about having people around me who cared about me—at least they seemed like they cared about me. It was about seeing Marco and Tristan loosen up even a smidge.

"We need another pitcher," Alice announced and she and Elodie headed back to the bar for more beer.

Tristan threw a strike and turned around like it was no big deal. I drank him in as he walked back. He was so good looking that I almost needed to look away sometimes for fear of being caught with my mouth gaping open. That electrical jolt I felt that first night I'd run into him buzzed to life, and I couldn't tear my eyes away from him.

Marco walked over to bowl next. Tristan eyed the vacant spot on the bench next to me. I held my breath, hoping he sat beside me. He, however, opted for the scorer's chair and sat with his back to me.

Did he not trust himself? Was he turned off by my tipsiness? Freaked out by my gawking? Or just as confused about our strange rollercoaster of a relationship as me?

Marco threw a strike before turning around with a smirk.

"Show off!" I called as I pushed myself to my feet, stepping past them both to get my ball. I felt their eyes on me, and I prayed I didn't throw a gutter ball. I approached the line, eyed the pins in their perfect triangle, and released the ball. It rolled straight all the way down the lane. "Come on, come on, come on," I murmured. The ball hooked left just before getting to the pins and hit one pin.

"Show off," Marco called.

I turned around and smiled. "All part of the game, my friend." I grabbed another ball and stood on the line again. I focused on the remaining pins and released the ball. It stayed straight all the way to the end and hit the front pin, knocking all the others down. *Spare!* My arms shot up as I spun to face them.

Marco shook his head, amused by my obvious excitement. When I looked to Tristan, he was grinning. I blinked hard, his grin nearly stopping me in my tracks. It was so foreign. So strange on his face. But at the same time, so beautiful and breathtaking.

I snapped out of my momentary haze and lowered my arms, walking back toward my seat. "That's how it's done boys," I said as I passed by them.

"Oh, is it?" Tristan said, almost playful.

I froze, scared that one of the other Tristans would return if I spoke.

"We're back!" Alice and Elodie called.

I turned my attention away from Tristan as Alice placed another pitcher of beer down on our table.

We spent the remainder of our time sharing the pitcher, getting worse at bowling, becoming a tiny bit sloppy…and a smidge too loud. My spare was a thing of the past and gutter balls were how I finished my night. Marco and Tristan didn't seem to mind though. They must've known I needed this.

On the car ride home, every time a new song came on the radio, one of us screamed out that it was our favorite song. We proceeded to sing the songs at the top of our lungs. At one point, Marco opened the window, likely trying to drown out our bad singing with the noise from the air outside. But we didn't care. We kept at it until we reached our dorm.

Tristan pulled to a stop in front of the entrance.

"I just want to thank everyone for celebrating my birthday with me," I said with a slight slur, hoping they all knew how much it meant to me. "This was a wonderful birthday." It might not have been the most conventional birthday, but nothing about my life had been conventional.

"*Awwwww.*" The girls wrapped their arms around me and squeezed me.

Neither Tristan nor Marco said anything, but at least they knew I appreciated them being there and making my birthday special.

Marco stepped out of the car and opened the back door. The three of us tumbled out, all giggling at our lack of balance. Marco stood there as we righted ourselves.

Elodie threw her arms around him and hugged him, causing him to freeze. "Thanks, big man."

"Be careful. He's got a gun," I whispered.

Elodie released him. Alice didn't seem to care about his weapon because she wrapped her arms around him next. "Thanks, sweet cheeks."

His grimace was hysterical.

I saved him the awkwardness by not touching him, instead joining the girls at the closed door.

Tristan drove off to park the car while Marco walked us into the building and escorted us upstairs. I said my goodbyes to the girls then Marco checked my bedroom so I could grab my toiletries. He checked the restroom before I washed up and brushed my teeth. Then we finally retreated to my room for one last sweep. He turned to leave.

"Thanks, Marco," I called to him.

"No problem, ma'am." He glanced back to me to see my reaction.

I flipped him off which earned me a chuckle before he closed my door, leaving me alone.

The sudden quiet caused an emptiness to creep into my chest that I hadn't felt all night. I slipped into my pajamas, wondering if I'd sleep since I'd had so much to drink. I also wondered if Tristan assumed the same thing and wouldn't come by.

As I climbed into bed, images from the night began to fill my head. And all of them involved Tristan. His breathtaking smile. His lack of annoyance at me and my drunk friends. The normal Tristan would've become all grouchy, but he seemed to let it roll off him, even finding it amusing at times.

I closed my eyes and was about to drift off to sleep when I heard my doorknob rattle.

Tristan

I unlocked Kresley's door and tiptoed into her room with the intention of just checking if she was asleep. As soon as I neared her bed, she rolled over, tucking her hands under her pillow and staring at me.

"Go to sleep," I said.

"Thank you for tonight, Tristan," she said for the second time that night, still with a slight slur in her speech. On any other girl, the slur would have been obnoxious, but it was kind of adorable on her, knowing what I knew about her.

I didn't respond because I *knew* she was appreciative. She didn't need to keep saying it.

"I know you didn't want to be there," she said, her voice growing quiet, like she was on the verge of falling asleep.

"I never said I didn't want to be there."

Her eyes absorbed the details of my face with droopy eyelids. "I know you better than you think," she said softly.

I scoffed, knowing she had no idea who I was or what plagued my mind when I slept. "Did you get everything you wanted for your birthday?"

She shook her head. "You didn't kiss me."

I flinched, her words yanking the rug right out from under me. Did she really want me to kiss her? Or, was she drunker than she seemed? I struggled to find the right words to respond. I didn't want to hurt her feelings, but rule number one was a real thing. It didn't matter, though. Because soft purrs of sleep escaped Kresley's lips, leaving me to consider her words. All. Fucking. Night. Long.

Dammit.

CHAPTER NINETEEN
Kresley

I was in a deep sleep when my phone began to ring on Saturday morning. The second I opened my eyes, I snapped them shut as the sun glared through the blinds. My mouth felt as if it were filled with cotton, so I smacked my lips to get rid of the feeling. But there was no getting rid of my slamming headache. I needed to rehydrate and pop some aspirin.

My phone was still ringing. I reached out for it and lifted it to my ear. "Hello?"

"Morning!" Elodie and Alice yelled at the same time.

"I think I'm dying," I grumbled.

"Not with that hot bodyguard sleeping in your room you're not," Alice said.

I glanced around. "Nope. No bodyguard here."

"We saw him go into your room," Elodie said.

I gasped, the events of the night slowly coming back to me. "Oh no."

"What?" they asked.

I cringed. "I think I asked him to kiss me."

They screamed.

I held the phone away from my ear.

"Did he?" Alice calmed down long enough to ask.

"I don't think so." I wracked my hungover brain trying to remember. "No, I definitely would've remembered him kissing me."

"You sure?" Elodie asked.

"I saw him staring at you in the rearview mirror the whole way home," Alice said.

"He was not," I said, though I had no idea if it was true or not; things were definitely a little foggy.

"I saw him too," Elodie added.

I didn't say anything, partially because I felt sick and partially because I didn't know what to do with that information.

"You wanna grab breakfast?" Elodie asked.

"I think I may vomit if I put anything in my stomach."

"Want us to bring you back a bagel and ginger ale?" Alice asked.

"Yeah. That would be good. Thanks."

We hung up and I reached over to place my phone back on my desk. My hand bumped something. I cracked my eyes open enough to spot a tall glass of water with two aspirin next to it.

Tristan.

I popped the aspirin into my mouth and took small sips of the water. Then, I yanked the comforter over my head and prayed that when I woke up again, I'd be rid of my headache and less embarrassed that I'd actually asked Tristan to kiss me.

* * *

Unsure if it was minutes later or hours later, knocking on my door woke me up. I thought about ignoring it, hoping if it was the girls, they would just leave my food in the hallway and let me sleep. But they kept knocking. "Leave it in the hall," I called.

The knocking continued.

Praying the room didn't spin, I sat up in my bed. When everything remained still, I pushed myself to my feet and went to the door.

"Kresley?" It was Chris.

I closed my eyes, scared to see what I looked like after the drunken night I'd had. "Hold on." I moved to the mirror and pulled my messy bed head into a knot on the top of my head. I licked my fingers and wiped the smeared mascara from beneath my eyes. Only then did I go open the door. "Hey."

Just like on our date, Chris looked nice *and showered* as his gaze travelled over my wrinkled tank top and bed shorts. "Did I wake you?"

"The girls and I went out last night." I pinched my fingers together. "I may have had a tiny bit too much to drink."

"I can come back."

I shook my head. "No, it's fine. What's up?"

"I was just visiting a friend upstairs and thought I'd see what you were up to, but I can see you're in rough shape."

"Tell me how you really feel," I joked.

"No, I just meant—"

"I was kidding. I know how I look and more so, how I feel."

He laughed. "There's this movie on the quad tonight—"

Tristan's door flew open and he stood there in just his boxers, glaring at us.

I cringed, knowing not only had he been up all night and was probably exhausted, but I'd also embarrassed myself in front of him big time. "Sorry. Did we wake you?"

"I had a long night," he said, his eyes boring into mine.

A shudder rushed through me, both embarrassed about what I'd said to him, but also kind of turned on that he was using code words for 'I had a long night because I was in *your* room all night.'

"Chris was just leaving," I blurted, feeling rude as soon as I said it.

"I was?" Chris asked me.

"Oh, well, I was gonna go back to bed," I explained, trying not to hurt his feelings.

"Want some company?" he joked.

Tristan growled low in his throat.

Nervously, I laughed a little too much for Chris' not-so-funny line. "I think I can handle it."

"Well, how 'bout I give you a call later?" Chris said. "You know, about that movie."

"That would be great," Tristan answered for me.

My brows pinched together, but I didn't dare look to Tristan. I focused on Chris. "It would," I agreed.

Chris looked from me to Tristan. "Aren't you her driver?"

Tristan closed his eyes and he pinched the bridge of his nose, seemingly pained to be having this conversation as opposed to sleeping. "I'm a lot of things. A driver. A brother. A bowler. Take your pick."

Chris looked back to me, thoroughly confused.

"Call me later," I said, before closing my door in both their faces.

I stood with my back pressed to the door, my breathing labored and my thoughts haphazardly rushing through my brain. I didn't want Chris to call me later.

I didn't want Chris at all.

I wanted Tristan.

And if I was being honest with myself, I think I'd wanted Tristan all along.

But was it just one-sided? Because the jealousy I saw in his eyes couldn't be my imagination. He had to feel something for me.

Maybe he just needed a little push to admit it to himself.

CHAPTER TWENTY
Kresley

There was loud banging at my door later that afternoon, and then I heard, "It's Marco."

I jumped off my bed and opened the door.

Marco's hands gripped my doorjamb and his chest rose and fell like he'd just run a race. "My wife was rushed to the hospital."

"That's great! Go!" I urged.

He shook his head. "Something's wrong with the baby."

My hands flew to my mouth. "Oh my God."

Tristan's door opened. "What's wrong?"

"She's having pain and that's all I know," Marco explained. "I called Briggs. He's on his way. But…"

"Go Marco," I said. "Go take care of your wife."

He nodded, his eyes wild with fear as they looked from me to Tristan.

"I got this," Tristan assured him.

"Thanks, man," Marco said. He tore his eyes away from Tristan and rushed down the hallway to the stairwell, disappearing without a second look.

Tristan and I stood in the hall, both shaken by a frazzled Marco. It was strange to see such a big bad man terrified. Neither of us were prepared for that.

"I'll stay in tonight," I assured Tristan.

His eyes searched mine, questioning my statement.

"So, you don't have to worry about getting extra security."

"You're to have at least two people available to you at all times," he explained.

I looked down, understanding protocol but finding it difficult to maintain eye contact with him. After the run-in earlier and my embarrassment over what I'd asked him, things were beyond awkward.

"You're gonna have to tell lover boy you can't see him tonight," Tristan said.

I glanced up at him. "What?"

"If you stay in, you won't be able to go to that movie."

Was he pushing me to be with Chris? Or, was he just curious to see my reaction? *Game on, bodyguard.* "That's okay. There are a lot of other things Chris and I can do in my room."

Tristan's eyes grew stormy, anger brewing in them.

Aha! Is that jealousy I see? "You could hang out with us if you'd like."

His face scrunched. "Why would I ever want to do that?"

I shrugged. "But, you'd obviously need to duck out if things…you know…heat up with Chris and me."

The ticking in his jaw said all I needed to know. Tristan Stone was jealous. Over *me.*

"Or…" I mused, trying to decide how to play this. "You and I could just hang tonight."

His eyes moved over my face, an internal war raging within him.

What's it gonna be, Tristan? "There's that movie on the quad Chris mentioned," I suggested.

"Do you know how difficult it is to protect you in a quad filled with people?"

My eyes moved to my bare feet, my lips twisting regrettably. I enjoyed pushing Tristan's buttons, but it suddenly wasn't fun anymore. Reality always had a way of reminding me that my life wasn't easy. "I'm sorry everything is so difficult when it comes to me."

He huffed. "It's not that."

I met his eyes. "Then what is it?"

He stared at me for a long time, his teeth dragging across his bottom lip. I couldn't tear my eyes from his. He stepped forward, moving toward my room. I stepped back. He brushed by me and walked inside.

I closed the door and turned to face him.

He continued to stare at me, his eyes moving over the cutoffs and T-shirt I now wore.

"What?" I asked, the silence and close proximity daunting.

"I didn't get you a birthday gift."

My brows knit together. "I don't need anything."

He stepped forward, causing me to step back. My back hit the door. I swallowed hard as Tristan's chest pressed to mine, his hands flat against the door above my head. My heartbeat began to slam against my ribs. I couldn't tear my eyes away from his. They were so damn blue and hypnotic as he gazed down at me from mere inches away. We'd never been this close and time seemed to stall.

"You asked me for something last night," he said, his voice low and gravelly.

I closed my eyes, embarrassed that my memory had been spot on.

"Do you remember?" he asked.

My eyes reopened and I nodded, embarrassment undoubtedly etched in my features.

His hands lowered from the door and cupped my cheeks. I stilled, stunned by his gentleness. His hands were soft on my skin as his eyes gazed down into mine.

"It was a request," I explained, my voice shaking with the sudden nerves overtaking my body. "And you said requests don't need to be—"

His lips crashed down on mine. His tongue pushed inside my mouth, not waiting to *request* access. I opened for him and his lips devoured mine in a frenzied race. The slide of his tongue sent my belly flipping over itself. *Holy shit. Tristan was kissing me!* My arms snaked over his shoulder as my heartbeat thrashed against my chest. My fingers tunneled through the back of his hair, pulling him closer. Now that I'd had a taste, I wasn't letting him go. I whimpered as I arched into him, my breasts pressing to his hard chest as he consumed every inch of my mouth. Our lips moved in sync, everything feeling so right. He was no boy struggling through a first kiss. He was a man taking what he wanted.

But all too soon, he pulled back.

Our chests heaved in tandem as we stared across the space between us. Oh. My. *God.*

"Happy birthday," Tristan said, before stepping around me and reaching for the doorknob.

I moved to the side, blocking his way, quite reminiscent of our first encounter. "You're kidding me, right?"

"What?"

"You're *leaving?*"

He said nothing, just stared at me.

"Let me guess. You're trying to convince yourself that you were just doing what I asked."

He shrugged, noncommittal.

"Bullshit."

Darkness flashed in his expression. "Is this really what you wanna do right now? You wanna pick a fight with me?"

I threw my hands out to my sides. "You started it the minute you tried to play it off as if you were just doing me some kind of favor and not what you wanted to do."

His eyes lifted to the ceiling as he dragged in a deep breath. "Whatever."

"Be *honest*, Tristan. Up until now, you were the *only* person who has been."

He cursed under his breath. "What do you wanna hear?"

"Oh, I don't know. The truth?"

A humorless laugh escaped him. "Right."

"What?" I persisted.

He shook his head, his exasperation palpable.

My heart wilted, hating the sudden turn of events. He just kissed me like he needed me in order to breathe, and now we were fighting. Par for the course with us.

"This is so fucked up," he murmured.

"What is?"

He stared at me, looking as though he was trying to convey so many thoughts with a single look. "Us."

The words tumbled out before I could stop them. "There's an us?"

He tunneled his fingers through his hair, ready to bolt from my room.

"You need to talk to me."

"What do you wanna hear? That I can't stop thinking about you even when I'm with you?" he asked.

His words punched the air right out of my lungs.

"That I can't fucking wait to come to your room every night even though I shouldn't be in here because I love watching you sleep?"

I stood dumbfounded as butterflies swarmed in my belly.

"That I wanna punch the shit outta Chris and anyone else who tries to get close to you because, by God, I can't be held responsible for my actions?"

I swallowed around the large lump that shot to my throat.

"Or, that it scares the hell out of me that people are out there who want to get to you?"

The ground beneath my feet shifted, both terrified by what he'd said but so damn happy that he'd said it. "I thought you hated me."

"I hated the way that you were working your way in here." He placed his hand over his chest. "And it's insane because there's absolutely no way this can work."

I ignored his words and stepped to him, slipping my hands around the back of his neck. "Shut up, Tristan." I drew his mouth to mine and our lips collided. I wasn't letting him push me away. I walked forward causing him to back up until his legs hit my bed. I pulled out of the kiss and pressed my palms to his chest, forcing him down onto my bed. He sat, waiting for my next move. I climbed onto his lap and cupped his cheeks. "You make me feel safe, Tristan."

His eyes drifted shut as if pained by my words.

"You sat outside my room because you knew I needed you to."

He opened his eyes and looked into mine.

"Then, you stayed in here because you knew I wasn't sleeping and your presence soothed me when nothing else in this world could."

His lips twisted, my candor unnerving him.

"You took me to a shooting range so I'd know how to protect myself if anything happened to you."

His mouth opened like he had something to say before slamming shut.

"And if we're being honest with each other, every time a girl looks at *you*, I want to shout from the rooftops that you sleep in *my* room so they'll stop looking."

The corners of his lips twitched.

"Every time you're around, I feel this pull to you that I've never felt before," I continued. "And I've tried to tell myself it wasn't real because you and I can't seem to get along for more than a few minutes at a time, but it *is* real, and I think you feel it too."

He didn't say anything, but the crinkle in his eyes told me he did.

"I've wanted you to kiss me since we ran into each other outside the men's room in the club, Tristan. So, freaking *kiss* me."

He smirked and I wanted to kiss it right off his face.

My hands slipped over his shoulders and to the back of his head. I ran my fingers through his hair, drawing his mouth to mine. He wasn't some unwilling participant. He kissed me back with the passion of every truth he'd admitted to me. My heart was light and my body quivered with need for him. I yearned to be closer. Yearned to feel every inch of him. I arched into him, and his erection pressed between my thighs. I couldn't stop myself from grinding against him as I kissed him with everything I had. Things were escalating, but I was *not* going to be the one to stop it—nor did I want to. But all too soon, Tristan pulled away. With both of us breathless, he shifted me off his lap and stood.

My pulse pounded in my temples. Was he having regrets? Was he leaving? I waited, willing him not to bolt again.

He didn't. He moved to the corner of my room, reached up to the camera, and pointed it up toward the ceiling. He spun back to face me sporting a sly grin.

"Now. Where were we?" He sat down and shifted me back onto his lap. His hands slipped to my back and under my tank top. I didn't have a bra on, so his big hands coasted over my skin as I leaned forward and pressed my lips to his. His fingertips left a trail of numbness in their wake and I tried committing every glorious touch to memory, wanting to remember the moment Tristan admitted he wanted me.

I normally wasn't so forward. So willing to shed my clothes. So desperate to be in someone's arms. But Tristan brought it out of me. I lifted my arms, and he pulled the hem right up and over my head, tossing it to the floor. I didn't have time to feel embarrassed by my nakedness. He leaned forward and flicked his tongue over my nipple. I closed my eyes, arching forward, unable to believe this was happening. Unable to believe *Tristan* was the one making my body feel alive. He moved to my other nipple and did the same.

"Tristan," I whispered as my head dropped back, relishing in the sensations.

"Yes?"

"Don't stop."

The raspy sound of his laughter disappeared once he sucked my nipple into his mouth. Tremors erupted between my legs as I braced my hands on his shoulders. He flicked his tongue again, biting down gently. I gasped. I could almost feel him smile against me before he tempered the sting with delicious swirls of his tongue.

He pulled back and peeled his shirt off. Underneath he was wearing a wife beater with holster vest over it. He unhooked the vest and placed it on my desk. Then he tugged off the wife beater.

I drank him in, all ripped and perfect. My hands drifted slowly over his chest, memorizing every dip and ridge before settling over his heart. His heartbeat drummed a steady rhythm beneath my palm.

"I want to feel you," he said, pulling my attention to his hungry eyes. "All of you."

I nodded, unable to tear my eyes from his.

He stood up while still holding me and turned, lowering me down onto the bed. He unbuttoned his jeans and pushed them and his boxers down, stepping out of them as I stared at him naked in front of me. His erection stood tall and thick. I'd been with guys before. But having Tristan naked in front of me was something else entirely. He was built and solid everywhere. I watched as he reached down and pumped his fist over his erection, looking directly at me. He smirked, likely at the heady look in my eyes. He eventually released his grip, using his hands to tug off my shorts and panties. I felt the heat of his gaze move over my naked body. The hunger in his stare ignited a fire beneath my skin. "I don't think a bad decision has ever felt so right." He crawled over me, spreading my legs with his knees.

"You think this is a bad decision?" I asked as he settled between my thighs.

"The worst."

My brows shot up.

"Too bad there's no turning back now," he said before capturing my lips. This kiss was unhurried, our tongues entwining in a slow intoxicating dance. Our naked bodies moved in sync, twisting together like magnets drawn to each other. Tristan shifted his hips and his erection pressed between my legs. I arched into him, suddenly needing more. He shifted his hips again, and our bodies continued their dance. Our kiss grew deeper. We were all teeth and tongues and getting very close to losing all sense of time. And, though we resisted the urge to go all in, prolonging the dance we'd been doing since the night we met, I needed Tristan. And I needed him now.

Sensing my impatience, Tristan abandoned my lips, burying his mouth in the crook of my neck. "Just think how good it's gonna feel…" he said as he whispered opened-mouthed kisses down the curve of my neck, branding my skin with the most delicious heat. "…when I'm inside of you."

The mere mention of him inside me sent tingles firing off everywhere. I bucked my hips, nearly impossible with the weight of him over me. But, he knew what I needed because he needed it too. He shifted his hips, pressing his dick against me harder this time. My eyes rolled into the back of my head, the sensations already so powerful. I was ready for him. I'd never been more ready for anything in my life.

He reached for his jeans on the floor and pulled a foil packet from his wallet, tearing it open with his teeth. He balanced on his side and rolled on the condom, then shifted back on top of me. "You're sure about this, right?"

"You're not, right?"

He smirked. "That smart mouth of yours is gonna get you in trouble."

"Oh, yeah? I didn't realize you were into the kinky stuff."

"I'm into you."

My stomach dipped, his words mixed with the sincerity in his eyes making me a complete goner. He leaned down and our lips collided once more. And while I knew he thought this was wrong, I was certain it was right.

Tristan thrust against me, preparing me without entering. He was unrelenting in his kisses as his hips thrust harder. He was ready, and he was making sure I was too. I bent my knees, my feet flat on either side of him as I lifted my ass. I held my breath as he pushed into me. I groaned as he stretched me wide. It took a second to adjust to the size of him, but once he began moving in and out, each time a little deeper, we found our rhythm. I matched each of his thrusts with my hips, loving the intimate connection between us.

"God, you feel amazing," he said between ragged breaths.

I loved his raw honesty. I wanted more. I dug my fingernails into his back and he groaned. I dragged them down to his ass. I kept my hands there, loving the feel of him flexing each time he thrust into me. He growled and wrapped one arm around my back, keeping us connected as he lifted me until I straddled him. I'd never done it in this position, so I gauged my moves on his reaction, moving my hips back and forth. "Just like that," he murmured, his eyes never wavering from mine as I rode him slowly. His hands drifted up and down my back, gently stroking my skin. Eventually, his fingers reached the back of my neck and he drew my mouth to his. Our tongues melded together as I moved on top of him, my hips shifting faster as our kiss grew deeper. Tingles began to build between my thighs, and my breathing became labored. I tore my lips from his and buried my forehead in his shoulder as my hips continued to move.

"Just like that, baby," he urged. "Just like that."

His words urged me on, and I could feel him thrusting from beneath me. He buried his mouth in the curve of my neck and sucked away at my skin as we moved together, a perfect dance between two no-longer-strangers.

Quivers began to coil around his dick, my body prepared to betray me. "Oh God," I groaned as the sensations released, rippling out to my limbs. My body shuddered as I rode out the orgasm.

Tristan didn't stop thrusting from beneath me, harder and deeper until he eventually stilled inside me, groaning against my neck as his own orgasm tore through him.

Our sweaty bodies stayed connected as we held each other, our breathing slowly leveling out and our heartbeats eventually returning to normal.

Oh. My. Freaking. God.

Tristan finally pulled back, his eyes taking in my face. He reached up and tucked strands of hair behind my ears. "Can we stay like this?"

My lips turned up in the corners, so happy he wasn't regretting this. "Happy? Or connected?"

"Both."

I smiled, loving this side of him. *This* Tristan. I leaned forward and kissed his sweaty lips. His dick twitched inside me, and I knew in that moment that he was having no regrets. I pulled back and gazed into his eyes. "Would taking a shower together draw too many questions?"

He laughed. "You think?"

"It's fine. I want your smell on me anyway."

"Damn right, you do."

We eventually broke apart and climbed under my comforter, with our clothes strewn across my floor.

Tristan wrapped his arms around me and pulled me into his chest. "You really want to fight every girl who looks at me?"

"You really watch me sleep?"

He nodded. "I love the way your eyelashes brush the tops of your cheeks."

"They do?"

He reached up and brushed his thumb over the top of my cheeks. "You look so peaceful. Like nothing can touch you while you're asleep."

"Nothing can if I know you're here," I explained. "If you're not…well, you know."

He dropped his lips to mine and kissed me slowly, his hands drifting down and around my hips, pulling me flush against him and holding me like he'd never let me go.

CHAPTER TWENTY-ONE
Kresley

"No…stop…please…"

Tristan's words yanked me from a sound sleep—again. His arms were wrapped around me from behind, but I knew he was asleep. His arms twitched as he pulled me closer to him. I couldn't see his face but felt the rigidity of his body as the words kept coming. "Please…no…"

I stroked my hand gently over his arm, trying to soothe him.

He startled, his heartbeat slamming against my back as he woke.

"You okay?" I whispered.

His arms dropped away from me, and he quickly rolled over and kicked his legs out from beneath my comforter.

I twisted to see what he was doing.

He sat on the edge of my bed naked with his back to me, running his fingers through his hair. "I fell asleep. *Again.*"

I sat up, holding the comforter around me and rubbing my hand over his back, trying to ease his mind. "It's fine."

He pulled away from my touch. "It's not fine," he snapped. "I can't protect you if I'm asleep."

I dropped my hand, feeling a sudden hollow in my chest. Was he mad at himself for falling asleep or mad at me for causing him to fall asleep?

He snatched his phone off my desk and checked it. "*Fuuuuck*," he said when he read a text on the screen. He stood, quickly gathering his clothes from my floor.

"What's wrong?"

He ignored me as he stepped into his jeans then tugged his shirt over his head. I waited for him to explain what was going on. Was it the text that upset him or the fact that he'd fallen asleep?

I suddenly couldn't keep up with his change in moods.

He snatched his holster from my desk. "I've gotta go."

"Go where?"

His eyes cut to mine. They were cold and detached.

The bastard was going to use falling asleep as a reason to push me away. "Don't do this," I warned with blood now pulsing in my cheeks.

He moved to the door.

I waited for him to stop and realize that he was overreacting. That he was going to ruin everything by walking out that door. I needed him to turn back around and tell me he was joking. Tell me everything he confessed earlier was the truth. Show me *that* Tristan.

He grabbed the doorknob.

I watched with bated breath.

He paused.

Come on, Tristan. Don't be a dick.

He twisted back around, but instead of facing me, he walked over to the camera in the corner of my ceiling that he'd repositioned earlier. He reached up and adjusted it back into place so it captured my room once again. He turned back to the door and, without another word, walked out.

The door clicked ominously behind him, piercing a dagger-sized hole in my already fragile heart.

Tristan

"Dude, what the fuck?"

I stopped short as soon as I stepped out of Kresley's room, not expecting to find Briggs waiting in the hallway, cross-armed and glaring at me.

"What?" I gritted.

"You and the client," he explained. "Rule number one."

"Don't fucking tell me rule number one," I growled. "I created it."

"Just stating the obvious," he said.

He clearly didn't know his place. I was the fucking boss! Why had Marco sent him? He was immature, a pain in the ass, and the least professional employee we had.

Fuck.

Look at me talking about not acting professionally when I just slept with the client. "I stay in her room at night," I clipped.

He pegged me with accusatory eyes.

"What?" I spat, pissed he was there. Pissed I'd fallen asleep. Pissed I'd had a nightmare in front of her again. Pissed I'd walked out on her the way I had. Pissed he was throwing my own God damned rule in my face!

"I saw you before you repositioned the camera and gave me a view of the ceiling," Briggs explained, his lips twitching.

My eyes narrowed as my anger flared to life. "What the fuck were you doing looking in her room?"

"You weren't answering your phone. And I wanted to be sure she was okay," he said. "But looks like you were making sure she was *just* fine."

My head fell back against the hallway wall, knowing what Marco and I drilled into our employees' heads. Rule number one. You don't fuck *or* fuck over your client. I thought I could handle it. I thought I was different and could make it work. I thought I could convince Marco I could have feelings for Kresley and still protect her. But I'd fallen asleep. *Twice.* Not to mention given her a front-row seat to my nightmares. *Twice.* I clearly hadn't been thinking with the head I should've been thinking with. "Marco's gonna kill me."

"Yup," he agreed.

"*Fuuuuuck.*"

Seconds felt like hours as my brain spun. I had absolutely no idea what I was gonna do to fix any of it.

"You know…" Briggs began. "I don't see why we have to burden Marco with this. He's got his own shit to deal with. And it's not like it's gonna happen again."

I looked at him as if my entire partnership with Marco—and everything we'd built—depended on Briggs keeping his big mouth shut and believing me. "It's not. It was a mistake."

"Good." Briggs turned and walked toward Marco's room where he'd be staying while Marco was gone. "I'm going to bed."

I stood alone in the hallway, contemplating what the hell to do. I couldn't get the feel of Kresley out of my head. She was three parts fragile and one part fierce. She was everything I needed to soften my hardened heart. But none of this was about *me*. I was there to keep *her* safe. And that wouldn't happen if I got too close. Despite everything I'd admitted to her earlier, nothing should've happened between us, especially under these circumstances. I knew better.

Maybe in a different time.

A different *life*time.

I turned to my room just as her door flew open.

Begrudgingly, I shifted my gaze to look at her, knowing what I'd find wouldn't be pleasant.

She glared at me. "It was a *mistake?*"

My eyes raked over her pajamas, knowing she'd just thrown them on since I'd left her naked in her bed. *God.* She looked so pretty and vulnerable. Like the girl I'd held in my arms for the last few hours. The girl I'd made love to. The girl I wanted to tell my secrets to. It killed me that I knew what she felt like. And tasted like. I shook off those thoughts and didn't say anything. Because nothing I said could justify my behavior.

"Is that really how you feel?" she asked, her lips in a tight line.

I didn't respond.

Disappointment filled her eyes. "So, this is how it's gonna be? After everything that was said, we're gonna go back to how things were with us hating each other? *Really?*"

I had so much shit flooding my brain that anything that came out of my mouth was bound to piss her off even more than she already was.

"Coward." She spun away from me with disgust in her tone and slammed her door, likely waking half the floor.

Coward?

That single word was like a sucker punch to my gut. I prided myself on being brave and running into danger as opposed to avoiding it. But when it came to Kresley, she'd been right. I ended up being the biggest coward of them all.

I lowered myself to the floor outside her room, knowing I needed to sit out there to keep her demons at bay. Little did I know at the start of the night that I would've become one of those demons now.

CHAPTER TWENTY-TWO
Kresley

I contemplated not going to the shelter the next morning. I considered staying in my room all day so I didn't have to face Tristan—so I didn't have to pretend things hadn't gone south in a matter of seconds. But why? Because he hurt my feelings? Because he turned his back on me? Because he was lying to himself?

I don't think so.

I was Kresley Hastings. I hadn't gotten to the place I was in by cowering in the face of adversity—as much as I might've wanted to at times. I'd escaped kidnappers, for Christ's sake. There was no way I was letting some bodyguard break me. If I'd been such a mistake, I was going to be a mistake that he had to face.

I opened my door.

Tristan waited in the hallway with his arms crossed and sunglasses on making it impossible to know if he was looking at me or not.

I wouldn't lie. The sight of him gave me a momentary pause as a rush of emotions flooded my chest. Regardless of the hurt I felt, I steeled my features and said nothing, just turned and walked down the hallway toward the stairwell.

"The car's out front," he said, as we walked down the stairs.

I quickened my pace. Immature? Maybe. But self-preservation was a powerful thing.

Outside the building, I opened the back door of the car and slipped into the backseat. No need to sit in the front to ignore him. I could manage just fine from the backseat.

Tristan rounded the front of the car. As soon as he opened his door, I focused on my phone in my lap. That would keep me busy until we arrived at the shelter. I skimmed through my newsfeed, but I wasn't paying attention to anything on the screen. My mind whirled with images of last night. How Tristan made me feel when he was telling me he couldn't stop thinking about me. The way his lips felt against mine, so soft and demanding. The way his body felt as he moved inside me. The safety I felt in his arms as we slept.

Then, as if a horrific car crash, everything flipped on its head. His nightmares. Him pissed at himself for falling asleep. Him calling our night a mistake.

And, as much as I wanted to tell him we could work through it all, I had too much pride to beg him to want me.

We arrived at the shelter amidst a blanket of dark clouds. The forecast didn't call for rain, but it would remain overcast—as if the heavens knew this day was going to suck. I opened my door before Tristan even shifted into park, needing to be far away from him.

I greeted Doris inside and headed to get my first three dogs. I stopped outside a cage with a new small black dog in it. "Doris? Who's this cutie?"

"Oh, that's Simone. She's quite a handful. A real yapper."

"Hello, Simone," I said to the black dog.

She barked.

"*Shhh*. It's okay. I'm gonna take you for a walk. Would you like that?"

She barked, but something about the way she did told me she was answering my question. I leashed her up as well as two other dogs then headed outside.

I avoided looking to where Tristan leaned against the car as the dogs headed straight toward the path. And, even with Tristan trailing somewhere behind me, walking in the woods gave me time to think. Time to reflect on what the hell happened between us. Tristan had been into it. He'd treated me the way I hoped to be treated by someone I cared about. He'd made me feel cherished. He made me feel wanted. He made me feel everything I knew he would. Then he had the nightmare, received the text from the bodyguard in the hallway, and all hell broke loose.

Rule number one. I got it. He wasn't supposed to be with me.

But if Tristan had been being honest about his feelings about me, there was no way he could've just shut them off because someone told him to.

Could he?

Well, I had news for him. If he was going to act like nothing happened between us, so was I. It was the only way to preserve my heart.

The drive back to campus was just as silent as the ride to the shelter. My eyes remained on my phone. A text from Chris popped on the screen. **Hey! What are you up to?**

Just driving back from volunteering. You?
Bored.

My thumbs fired off a text. **Want some company?**

His response was immediate. **Yes! Wanna come by the frat house?**

I glanced to the rearview mirror. Tristan's eyes were on the road. I sent off my reply. **Be there in ten minutes.**

I'll wait outside.

I smiled, knowing this would piss off Tristan. Not only was it not pre-planned for security measures, but it showed him that I didn't need him. If he could shut his feelings down, I was gonna try damn hard to do it too. "Bring me to Sigma Chi," I said to Tristan without meeting his eyes in the rearview mirror.

"No."

"You work for me," I clipped. "And I said I want to go there."

"I'm not your chauffeur."

I met his gaze in the mirror. My eyes narrowed, and I hoped the hurt and anger I felt was conveyed through them. "I'll walk."

"I'm not escorting you there."

"Do I look like I need you or your permission?"

His eyes cut away and focused back on the road.

"Briggs can take me. That's his name, right? The guy you told I was a mistake."

He said nothing and when we pulled through the front gates of campus and through fraternity row, I wondered if he'd relent. He didn't.

"Stop the car!" I demanded as we passed Sigma Chi.

"Nope."

Chris sat out front on the porch waiting for me, not even realizing I was being held captive by a surly bodyguard. "I hate you."

Tristan didn't respond, which just pissed me off more.

"You can't not want me, Tristan, but then stop me from seeing someone who does."

He still said nothing.

"I need friends. I need people who want to be around me. I need normal in my life. You can't stop me from having that."

He pulled to a stop in front of my dorm.

I threw open the door and jumped out, walking in the opposite direction of the entrance. I was not trying to be immature, but he was pushing me by not being honest with me *or* himself. I'd go to the fraternity. I'd spend time with a guy who wanted to spend time with me. I'd erase Tristan Stone from my brain forever.

I yelped as I was lifted right off my feet.

"Knock this shit out," Tristan said as he threw me over his shoulder.

"Put me down," I said through gritted teeth as heads turned as we moved by a group of students standing outside the building.

"No."

Anger pulsed through me and tears stung my eyes as he carried me to the entrance of the dorm and scanned his card. Why was he doing this? He was the one who needed to knock it off. He wasn't being fair. He didn't want me. He didn't care about my feelings. But now he was going to go all caveman on me. This was messing with my head and my heart. Didn't he realize that?

"Put me down," I demanded.

"Will you go up to your room?" he asked.

"Do I have a choice?"

He released a breath before lowering me to my feet.

I righted myself before climbing the stairs to my floor. I walked ahead of him down the hallway and stopped at my door, knowing the drill but hating that I had to spend another second near him.

He entered my room and checked it before walking back out into the hallway. He turned to face me like he had something to say.

I walked into my room and slammed the door in his face. I moved to my bed and dropped face first onto it. I lay there for a long time, hating that I was trying to make Tristan jealous. Hating that my pillow still smelled like him. Hating him for treating me like I was just a one-night stand. Hating that he told the new bodyguard that what happened was a mistake. *I* was a mistake.

There was a knock on my door a little while later. I pushed myself up from my bed, cursing myself for wanting it to be Tristan. Wanting him to tell me the truth. I moved to the door and waited for him to speak.

"Kresley? You in there?" It was Chris.

Shit. I'd never texted to let him know I couldn't come by.

I opened the door, half expecting Tristan to be frisking him, but Chris stood alone and Tristan's door remained closed. He must've been in the shower because caveman Tristan would've been out there if he knew Chris had come by. I looked to Chris hoping he could see the regret on my face. "I'm so sorry. My driver was having a bad day and refused to take me over. I came in here and…fell asleep." I was a terrible liar.

His eyes narrowed, clearly not buying my excuse.

"Come in." I stepped back. "You wanna watch a movie or something?"

His lips pulled into a smile, my indiscretion quickly forgotten. "Sure."

I closed the door and moved to my bed, straightening the comforter where I'd thrown myself down earlier.

"How was volunteering?" he asked.

"Good. There's a new dog that's super cute." I sat down on my bed with my back against the wall and my legs stretched out in front of me. I patted the spot beside me so he knew it was okay to sit on my bed. "What should we watch?"

Chris slipped off his shoes and sat beside me. We skimmed through the titles on Netflix on my laptop. "Oh, have you seen *Money Heist?*"

I shook my head.

"It's dubbed, but it's awesome. Totally binge-worthy."

We turned it on and spent the next three hours watching it. He was right. It was awesome. But I couldn't shake the emptiness in my chest about what happened with Tristan. And I couldn't shake the thoughts that I wished it was Tristan beside me doing normal college stuff instead of Chris.

"You getting hungry?" Chris asked. "We could get a pizza."

"Sure."

"How do you feel about Hawaiian?"

"Never had it. But I'm open to trying new things."

He ordered the pizza then we watched one more episode of the show before there was a knock on the door.

"Who are you?" Tristan's deep voice carried through my door from the hallway.

Shit.

I jumped off the bed and hurried to the door, throwing it open.

Tristan looked to me with daggers as he held the delivery guy's arm. "Forget to tell me something?"

I ignored him and looked to the delivery guy. "Jeff!" I was so glad to see a friendly face, but he looked totally confused. "I'm so sorry about him." I took the pizza box from Jeff's hand. "How much do we owe you?"

"We?" Tristan asked just as Chris stepped into my doorway. His gaze dropped to Chris' bare feet and then cut to my eyes. Anger stewed in his gaze.

Jeff's eyes jumped wearily from Tristan to Chris to me. Then he burst into laughter. "It's already paid for," he assured me, his wide eyes showing intrigue.

"Oh. Great. I'll see you Monday in class," I said, shooting him a look that hopefully conveyed that I'd fill him in then. I spun around and walked into my room.

Chris followed me in, shutting the door behind us and leaving Tristan standing alone in the hallway. "What's really going on with that guy?"

I grabbed a slice of pizza from the box, took a bite, then sat cross-legged on my bed. "Do we really have to talk about him?" I asked with a mouthful.

Chris sat in my desk chair, the one Tristan usually occupied. "No." He grabbed a slice. "But I'm starting to have some questions."

I nodded, understanding why he would.

"It's more than just your parents being cautious, isn't it?" he said.

"Yeah."

"Are you in some kind of trouble?"

I shrugged. "I could be."

"Is there anything I can do to help?"

"I think I've got it covered in that department."

His eyes drifted to my closed door as if looking to Tristan's room.

I nodded my answer to his unasked question.

And then that was it. He let it go. At least for the time being.

We shared the pizza then he moved back onto my bed, where we watched another couple of episodes of the show.

Somewhere around midnight, my eyelids became heavy, and I found it difficult to keep them open. My head tilted onto Chris' shoulder, and I felt myself slowly drifting off. Maybe I didn't need Tristan. Maybe I just needed to know someone was there...

Visions of my apartment in France manifested. I saw myself standing alone in my room. Blood covered my shaking hands. I called for Andre but he didn't come. Tears fell from my eyes. A masked man stepped into my doorway. His heavy footsteps echoed like a drum. He circled me, but I couldn't move. My feet were stuck to the floor. I struggled to get them free but they wouldn't budge. "*Le fou de fortune*," he whispered. Then his voice grew louder. And louder. I lifted my hands to my ears but it wouldn't block out the sound. "*This isn't over*," he said as he stepped in front of me. I could see blood soaking his mask, the smell burning my eyes.

I screamed out, my body jolting upright.

But I wasn't in France. I was sitting in my dorm room with my heart thrashing in my chest and sweat drenching my shirt. And Chris was still sitting beside me.

His eyes were wide with fear. "Are you okay?"

My door sprang open and Tristan rushed in. In one swift movement, he grabbed Chris off the bed by his neck and slammed him against my now closed door.

"What the hell are you doing?" Chris cried, struggling against his grip.

"What did you do to her?"

"Nothing," Chris said, his voice rising with fear.

"Tristan, stop it! I was having a dream."

He didn't look at me. He kept his hand and eyes on a terrified Chris. "You need to get your things and go home," Tristan said, his tone calm yet menacing.

"Tristan, let go of him!" I climbed off my bed and rushed to them. "Now!"

He reluctantly released Chris and stepped back.

"I'm so sorry about this," I said to Chris as he gathered his shoes and shoved his feet into them.

"It's late anyway," he said, though I knew he was embarrassed by the ridiculous turn of events.

"I had fun," I said, trying to reassure him though I was still reeling from the nightmare I'd just had.

His eyes shot to Tristan. "Yeah." Chris moved to the door and Tristan stepped back as he opened it.

I followed Chris into the hallway. "I really am sorry."

"You have nothing to be sorry about. I'm sorry you had a bad dream."

"Yeah."

He moved forward and pressed his lips to my forehead. "I'll call you."

I wanted the intimate gesture to elicit feelings in me. Warmth. Desire. Need. But it didn't, falling so much flatter than the jolt of electricity accompanying Tristan's lips anywhere on my body.

Once Chris disappeared into the stairwell, I turned back to my room prepared to face Tristan. I stormed inside only to find him in my desk chair with his face in his palms.

"I'm sorry you were having a nightmare," he said.

"Yeah, well, you should've considered that before you barged in my room." I moved to the closet and pulled off my now-sweaty clothes, tossing everything into my laundry bag hanging inside. I had no idea if Tristan was looking. But I welcomed it. *Look at what you could've had if it hadn't been such a mistake.* I pulled on a tank top and pajama shorts then opened my door and stepped into the hallway. "I need to brush my teeth."

I walked to the bathroom and waited outside with my arms crossed, waiting for Tristan to arrive.

When he finally did, I could feel his eyes on me, but so much hurt and confusion filled me, it was better not to look at him.

As he searched the bathroom, my chest tightened around my racing heart, hating him for kicking Chris out even though he knew I'd had a nightmare. A nightmare that could have been prevented if he hadn't abandoned me.

When he stepped back out, I walked around him, careful not to touch him. I walked inside and intentionally took my time. He could wait.

When I finished in the bathroom, I found him leaning on the wall outside my room. I walked in and Tristan followed me. I spun around, holding up my palm to stop him. "You can stay in the hall."

"*Kresley*," he said, his voice soft and concerned. "Your nightmare."

"Not your concern." I turned away, moving to my bed and slipping under my comforter.

He paused like he wanted to say something. But there was nothing left to say. I had a nightmare because *he* wasn't there. He knew it and so did I.

Apparently, that wasn't enough to make him admit he'd been wrong. Admit he was being a coward.

He turned toward the door and opened it. He didn't pause this time. He switched off my light and stepped out into the hallway.

The door clicked shut behind him, and only then did I allow the tears to fall.

CHAPTER TWENTY-THREE
Kresley

Briggs was out in the hall waiting for me Monday morning. And while I should've been pleased not to see Tristan, my heart wilted. But I pulled it together. I would not feel let down. I was so much tougher than that. So much *smarter* than that. I didn't need a guy who didn't want me. "You ready for college?" I asked Briggs as we made our way out of the building.

"Ready as I'll ever be," he said.

I laughed. He was young like Tristan, so he probably skipped college and went right into the security business. "Watch out for college girls. They see fresh meat and pounce."

He snickered. "I think I can handle college girls."

"You say that now."

We walked the rest of the way in silence. Briggs was a good-looking guy with a buzz cut resembling someone in the military. He was stocky, not as tall or built as Tristan, but he still had that edge needed to work security.

"Any word on Marco's wife?" I asked him.

"She's still being monitored, but the doctors say she's doing okay."

I made it to my first class and Briggs waited in the hallway. As much as I wanted to dislike him for all but telling Tristan that he and I were a bad idea, I understood he was just trying to get him to do the right thing for his business. Dating a client was a bad idea. Tristan had said so himself.

"So, you said you had a few options," Jeff said as soon as I arrived to accounting class later. "But I didn't realize they were ready to throw down for you."

"Oh, God, what a nightmare. I'm so sorry about that," I said, closing my eyes as recollections of the scene flashed through my mind.

"That dude grilled me like he thought I was some kind of pizza-carrying ninja ready to fight him."

I cringed, hating that this was my life. "Yeah, he's a little…intense."

"I'd say…So, which one's your man?" he asked, brushing it off like those kinds of things happen to him all the time.

"Neither," I said.

"Yeah, right."

The professor entered the room and our conversation thankfully came to an end.

***

Briggs accompanied Elodie, Alice, and me to the dining hall for dinner. Where had Tristan been? Had he asked not to see me or had it been recommended that he take a break?

"So…Chris?" Alice asked.

"We binged a Netflix show and ate some pizza," I explained.

"Yeah, so your text said *last* night," Elodie added. "But we heard a commotion in the hallway *Saturday* night."

"Marco's wife got rushed to the hospital and he needed to leave quickly."

Their eyes widened.

"Is she okay?" Elodie asked.

"I think so. Marco sent Briggs in his place," I explained.

"We didn't hear Marco. We heard Briggs," Alice clarified. "He was reaming out Mr. Hottie for being in your room."

Elodie and Alice had certainly missed a lot. But I was too embarrassed to share that we'd slept together then he called it a mistake. "You guys know Tristan stays in my room. In a *chair*."

"Sounded like Briggs knew something," Elodie said.

"Sounded like there was *something* going on," Alice added, her brows raised in question.

"Did you guys have your ears to the door?" I asked.

"*No!*" they said in unison.

"We had the door cracked," Alice admitted.

We all laughed because it was so typical of them to be in my business. I seriously needed to find them guys to occupy their time. Jeff and Chris were single. I glanced over at Briggs, standing there in sunglasses even though it was evening—and we were inside. Maybe *he* was single.

"Are you and Chris hanging out again?" Alice asked.

The recollection of last night's incident brought on a cringe.

"What?" Elodie asked, sensing me holding back.

"Tristan kicked him out of my room."

"That's awesome," Alice said way too loud.

I covered my face, hoping my hands somehow shielded me from all the looks our table was receiving.

"You coming here has been the best thing ever!" Alice proclaimed.

"We are totally living vicariously through you," Elodie added, like I didn't already realize that.

I dropped my hands from my face. "You do realize I'm here because I'm supposed to be laying low, right?"

They nodded, the sense of danger no deterrent for these two.

I wished I had their bravery.

* * *

Once I was alone in my room again, I worked on a couple of assignments on my laptop before filling in my parents on volunteering and my classes. They told me Marco should be back by the weekend which gave me a small sense of peace.

Around ten, Briggs accompanied me to the bathroom then checked my room for the night. I flipped off my light and climbed into bed. I felt myself dozing off a short time later, but only after I heard shuffling on the other side of my closed door.

Tristan.

In the hallway.

Following my request to stay out of my room.

* * *

I didn't see Tristan for the entire week. Briggs walked me to my classes and was on dinner duty, along with bathroom checks. But, once my door was closed for the night, I always knew Tristan sat out in the hallway.

Not surprising, Chris hadn't called. I guess I was more trouble than I was worth.

When the girls suggested going to the bar Friday night, I knew Tristan wouldn't be able to hide any longer. Drawing him out of hiding was the only thing that gave me motivation to go since I really wasn't in the mood to party. I let Briggs know we were going so he and Tristan could handle the logistics on their side.

I spent way too much time in the mirror, changing numerous times until I knew I looked my best in short black shorts, a silk fuchsia halter top, and the highest black Louboutin heels I owned. I was going to show Tristan what he was missing out on if it was the last thing I did.

We left the dorm at ten with Briggs leading the way outside. My steps faltered when we reached the SUV. The bodyguard who helped Briggs at the bowling alley sat in the driver's seat. Not Tristan.

Where was he? Was he already at the bar? Or, had he been taken off my assignment?

"Turn it up!" Alice yelled as soon as the bodyguard started the car and a song she liked played on the radio.

"Is Tristan already at the bar?" Elodie leaned forward and asked Briggs in the passenger seat.

I wished I didn't care. I *really* wished I didn't care. But, my ears perked up.

"He's got the night off," Briggs said.

My entire body deflated as the words left his mouth. Tristan had made a fool of me. Made me feel something for him only to cast me aside. Now I was dressing up to make him feel bad for not wanting me, and he wasn't even going to be there. God. I was so pathetic.

We arrived at the bar, and I plastered on a smile, not wanting to show anyone my disappointment.

Briggs led the way inside while his partner followed us from behind. Briggs made his way through the crowd to a table on the far side of the bar that had a *Reserved* sign on it.

"We'll be nearby," Briggs informed me over the music. "Just signal one of us over if you need anything."

I nodded, before the girls and I settled on stools at the round high-top. We ordered shots and spent a good hour at our table laughing and talking before heading to the dance floor. Regardless of my initial disappointment, I needed to have fun with the girls. So, I let the thought of Tristan flee my brain and I let loose, dancing until we were drunk and sweaty and didn't care who was watching us.

"Tristan's here!" Alice shouted over a song.

My head whipped around, checking the corners of the room. I didn't see him. I spotted Briggs who watched the crowd intently. I looked back to Alice. "Where?"

She pointed toward the bar.

I searched the bar area which was two people deep all the way around, finally spotting him at a corner seat. I stilled. A blonde scantily clad girl sat beside him, leaning into his side and whispering in his ear.

Heat pulsed in my cheeks and my stomach roiled. Without a word to Elodie or Alice, I pushed my way off the dance floor. I needed to get to the bathroom. I needed to catch my breath. He'd done this on purpose. He knew I was jealous of other girls and purposely brought one with him.

There was a long line for the girl's bathroom, so I stormed right into the men's room. The guys standing at the urinals didn't seem to mind, laughing when they spotted me over their shoulders.

I pushed my way into the only stall and braced my hands on the walls, gasping for air.

I needed to breathe.

I needed to think.

I needed to erase the vision of Tristan and that girl from my mind.

"You all right in there?" one of the guys asked.

"I'm fine," I lied.

"You sure?" came another voice.

I dragged in one last breath and opened the door to the stall. "That girl's line is just way too long," I said with a grin.

The guys smiled as I attempted to steadily make my way to the hand sanitizer by the door. Truth be told, I would've been steadier on a trapeze. I washed my hands then yanked open the door, almost falling back when Tristan stood there glaring at me.

I straightened my spine and tipped up my chin. "Move," I said.

He didn't, his broad chest remaining in my face. I wished I didn't know what that chest felt like beneath my hands or how strong it felt when pressed to mine while he was thrusting inside me.

"She said move," one of the guys behind me said.

I kept my chin lifted in defiance.

Tristan's eyes remained locked on mine, but he eventually relented, stepping back so I could walk out.

It took everything in me not to make a dig about the blonde at the bar, but I'd made plans with Chris, so I really had no right. And in my drunken stupor, I was bound to say way more than I should.

The guys in the men's room walked me toward the dance floor before going their separate ways.

I was about to step back out onto the dance floor when someone grabbed my arm and tugged me back. I spun around, coming chest to chest with Tristan. "Let go," I said through clenched teeth.

He didn't release me.

I cocked my head, tears threatening to pool in my eyes. I willed them back. "What do you want from me?"

He stared at me long and hard, his lips twisting regrettably.

His silence kept my tears at bay, pissing me off instead of making me sad. "I get it, Tristan. You're here to make a point. I get it. We're never happening. Message received."

His eyes dropped away from mine, and he let go of my arm.

Coward.

I spun away from him and went back to the dance floor, pushing my way to Elodie and Alice. "You guys ready?"

They could see the urgency in my face because they didn't hesitate, following me toward the exit. Briggs and his partner met us outside and walked us to the car. We slipped into the backseat, and the girls knew enough not to ask what was wrong. Briggs drove us back to the dorm. It was a quiet ride, but only because Elodie and Alice fell asleep.

I'd sobered up dramatically after the run-in with Tristan and the sight of him with someone else.

I woke the girls at the dorm, and Briggs helped them out of the car.

"Piggyback?" Alice asked him.

"No," Briggs said, though he stifled a smile.

"No fun," she slurred.

Briggs' partner parked the car while Briggs helped get them upstairs. We used the bathroom then said our goodnights. After Briggs checked my room, I slipped into my pajamas and climbed into bed. I felt sick for more than one reason.

Sometime in the middle of the night, my door opened and closed. Tristan's crisp scent filled my room and I sensed him sit down in the chair. I was too angry and exhausted to say anything. I lay there for a long time, hating him. Or, at least trying to.

"I know you think this is easy for me," he said softly. "Having to be around you."

"You're fired," I said. "There. Now you can go home."

"I'm not joking, Kresley."

"Neither am I, Tristan."

"I'm trying to do the right thing," he said.

"For who? You? Me? Your employees?"

I could hear him push the chair back and stand. "This was a bad idea."

I rolled over in my bed so I could finally face him. "You mean a mistake?"

He stared at me, exhaustion heavy in his features.

"Dammit, Tristan. Stop lying."

"About what?"

"Everything."

His eyes stayed on mine for a long time. I willed him to be honest. I willed him to tell me the truth. I thought he was going to, but instead, he resorted to his cowardly ways. "Good night." He turned and walked out of my room.

I listened, waiting for his door to open, but it didn't. Had he left? Had he finally taken me at my word that he was fired?

Then I noticed his shadow lingering outside my door, and I knew he sat in the hallway.

I wished he hadn't. I *really* wished he hadn't. Because it just made me think he still cared—even just a little bit.

CHAPTER TWENTY-FOUR
Kresley

I didn't see Tristan at all on Saturday, just his shadow outside my room that night. But, Sunday morning, he was leaning against the hallway wall when I opened my door to go volunteer. My feet caught on the floor, not expecting to find him there decked out in black on black. I wondered if it was a show of defiance since he knew how much I hated it.

We walked in silence to the car. I slipped into the backseat and pulled out my phone, using it as a distraction for the ride. I would not look at him. I would not speak to him. He did this. Not me.

Once we arrived at the shelter, I pushed open the door and hurried in to see Doris and the dogs. I grabbed Simone and two other pups and leashed them. I averted my gaze as I moved by Tristan who stood against the car.

A dark blanket of clouds covered the sun as we set off on our walk. Since I wore cutoffs and a hoodie, goosebumps scampered up my legs as a cold chill moved through the woods. And, as much as I tried not to think about last night's conversation between Tristan and me, it was all I could think about as his footsteps trailed behind me.

Why wasn't it easy for him to be around me?

Did he think it was easy for *me*?

His footsteps stopped as I paused to let the dogs sniff their favorite tree. After a couple of minutes, I continued walking deeper into the woods but I didn't hear Tristan behind me. Good riddance. I began to hum and the dogs' tails went crazy, wagging at the sound of my humming. I laughed, loving how dogs' love was unconditional.

"Kresley!" Tristan called from a distance.

Footsteps pounding the ground echoed through the woods behind me.

I spun around, ready to give Tristan a piece of my mind. But it wasn't him.

A man in a dark hoodie rushed toward me. Alarm bells wailed in my head as the hair on the back of my neck stood on end. I dropped the leashes and spun away from him, running as fast as I could deeper into the woods. I stumbled over tree roots as my heartbeat ricocheted off my chest, but I stayed upright because I knew I needed to get away from this man. Every step I took felt like it was happening in slow motion. Tree branches tore at my clothes as I plowed off the path and into the thick brush and darkness of the woods. I wouldn't turn around. I just needed to run. Run as if my life depended on it. Because it *did*. Tears burned my eyes as I propelled my legs forward, hearing the footsteps behind me getting closer.

A gunshot reverberated through the woods.

I dropped to the ground and covered my head. A scream I couldn't contain tore out of me. My limbs shivered as I mentally assessed myself for pain. My head. My back. My arms. My legs. I didn't feel anything. My head jerked over my shoulder.

Tristan, with a gun in his hand, stood over the man who now lay face down on the ground no more than twenty feet away from me.

Complete terror washed over me and tears rolled down my cheeks as what happened finally registered.

Tristan looked anxiously to me. "Are you hurt?"

"I'm okay," I called, my voice cracking.

He leaned down and quickly zip-tied the man's hands and ankles, but the pool of blood beneath him told me he was no longer a threat.

I crawled to my knees. Physically, except for a few bloody scrapes marring my knees and elbows, I was fine. Mentally, I wasn't sure I'd recover.

Tristan rushed over to me, his eyes assessing me while still staying alert of our surroundings. "I need to check the perimeter. But I need to know you're safe in the car." He held out his hand to me. "Come on. I don't know if he was alone."

Fear gripped me, knowing there could be more men out there. I grabbed his hand and he pulled me to my feet.

"Stay behind me," he said, easing me behind him. He walked with his gun extended in front of him and his head moving from side to side, his eyes undoubtedly scanning the wooded area around us.

Neither of us spoke as we moved toward the start of the path that seemed miles away, our ears alert for unfamiliar sounds. There were so many places someone could hide in the cover of the woods. So many places someone could lay in wait with a gun aimed at my head. I jumped every time a branch snapped beneath our feet. And, the jackhammer pounding in my chest soon blocked out all other noises.

"Almost there," Tristan assured me.

Once we could see the clearing, Tristan rushed me to the car, throwing open the back door and helping me inside. "Get on the floor and stay down."

I did as told, shaking uncontrollably as he closed the door and locked me inside.

Minutes felt like hours as I lay on the floor of the backseat, trembling as if hypothermia had set in. How had that man found me? How had he gotten by Tristan? Who else knew where I was? Who else was coming?

I could hear dogs barking inside the shelter. I'd let go of the dogs. I'd left them to fend for themselves. And, poor Doris. I hoped Tristan told her to lock herself inside.

Sirens bellowed in the distance and relief washed over me as they moved closer. Tires sped up the dirt road and the sirens grew louder; the dogs inside the shelter began to howl. When the sirens stopped, I heard doors open and slam shut then footsteps pounding on the ground. Police officers seemed to spread out in every direction. I heard voices outside the car. I could finally breathe. The cavalry had arrived.

I pushed myself to my knees and peeked out the tinted windows. Police officers scoured the area. EMTs ran into the woods with a stretcher. Briggs jogged around checking the perimeter of the woods.

I pushed open the back door and hurried to the shelter wanting to make sure Doris was okay. She didn't ask for any of this. I'd brought danger to her sanctuary. I tried the knob, but the door was locked. *Good.* I knocked on the door. It took a minute, but Doris peeked through the window, her eyes wide with fear. When she saw it was me, she unlocked the door and I pushed my way inside, locking the door behind me. "Are you okay?"

She nodded, visibly shaken. "Are *you* okay?"

"I'm fine. But I had to let Simone and the boys go."

"They're already back in their cages."

I breathed a sigh of relief. "Thank God."

"Was anyone hurt?" she asked.

I nodded. "He was after me. And my bodyguard shot him before he hurt me."

"Oh, honey. Why would someone want to hurt you?"

I peeked out the door. Tristan stormed toward the car—the one I was no longer in. "Doris, I've gotta go outside. But I promise I'll explain."

"Is it safe out there?"

"I hope so." I ducked out the door and heard the lock click as I headed toward Tristan, ready for him to ream me out for leaving the car.

Anger clouded his eyes as he approached me. But instead of yelling at me, he wrapped his arms around me and held me to his chest.

I felt myself melt into him, needing the safety of his arms more than I ever imagined. Tears stung my eyes.

He tightened his arms. "I've never been so scared in my entire life. If I ever lost you…"

Lost me?

But he didn't want me.

"…I don't know what I'd do if anything happened to you."

"You shot someone…" I swallowed. "…for me."

"I thought he was gonna get to you," he said.

I closed my eyes, realizing how close I'd come to being hurt or taken. "I'm okay. Are you okay?"

He pulled back and stared into my teary eyes. "Am *I* okay? *Seriously?*"

I nodded, terrified that either of us could've been hurt.

He leaned forward and pressed his lips to mine, kissing me slow and purposeful. Even if this was just the shock of what happened, I still let him kiss me. I needed him and wanted to melt into the kiss, needing it more than I needed air. Needing *him* more than I needed air. He pulled back and dropped his forehead to mine. "I'm so damn sorry I let him get by me."

"I heard you call out. I knew to run."

His eyes pinched tightly. "I should've been walking with you. I was giving you your space when all I really wanted to do was be in it."

I said nothing, knowing I had a lot to do with the reason he was keeping his distance.

"Listen, I've gotta go explain why there's a dead body in those woods." He gave me a reassuring nod as he released me and stepped back. "Lock yourself in there with Doris. I won't be long." He turned to walk away.

"Tristan?" I called.

He stopped and looked back. "We'll talk when I'm done, okay?"

I nodded and then he was gone.

I spent the next thirty minutes assuring Doris no one would be back to the shelter to hurt her. *I hoped.* Then, two detectives came in and questioned us. Doris said she hadn't seen anything, and I told them everything I knew, which wasn't much since most of the time I was running for my life.

Eventually, they left and Tristan returned. I said goodbye to Doris and stepped outside to join him. The remaining police cars drove by, kicking up clouds of dust as they drove down the dirt road and away from the shelter.

"Everything all set?" I asked Tristan.

He wrapped his arms around me and pulled me into his chest, holding me tight like he had before. "God, I hope so."

Being in his arms brought back so many emotions...so many thoughts of our night together.

How strong he was. How safe I felt with him near me. But what was really going on? Had this intense situation made him realize that I hadn't been a mistake? *Or,* had it made him think irrationally and he'd go back to being the cold Tristan tomorrow?

He walked me to the passenger door of the car and helped me in. Before I could turn, he stood between my knees in the open door, just looking at me.

"What?"

"I lied," he said.

My brows shot up. "About what?"

"Nothing that happened between us was a mistake."

All the tension I felt from the past week released from my body.

"I've never had feelings for a client before," he continued. "There are rules in place for a reason."

I nodded, understanding that being in a relationship with me could cause him to be distracted.

Fear clouded his eyes. "What if I'd missed today and he got to you? What if I didn't see him and he took you away? What if—"

I stroked his cheek. "You didn't miss. And you did see him. I'm okay because of *you*, Tristan. *You* protected me." I tilted my head, taking in his worried eyes. "*You* saved me."

He closed his eyes, the truth showing his vulnerability and affecting him in a way I'd never seen before.

"You were wrong when you told me you weren't a superhero," I said as his eyes reopened. "Because right now I feel like you're my very own."

He opened his mouth to respond—probably to tell me I was wrong—but I cut him off.

"Please get in the car," I said. "And take me back to the dorm where you can protect me some more."

He shot me a sad smile and nodded. I shifted my legs into the car and he closed the door. I watched him round the car before he slipped into the driver's seat and linked his hand with mine. It was as if he needed the contact and needed to be sure I was okay. He started the engine and pulled out onto the dirt road.

I noticed Briggs in the car behind us following us away from the shelter.

"Tristan?"

He glanced to me.

"*Are* you okay?"

He looked back to the road. "Yeah, I'm good."

"I'd understand if you weren't. You just killed someone."

"Someone who would've hurt *you*."

"Yeah, but—"

He shook his head. "I promise. I'll be able to sleep at night knowing he can't hurt you now."

I understood his rationale. That man wasn't a good man. He was someone paid to get to me. Someone who willingly took money *to* get to me. Would he have kidnapped me? Shot me in the leg so I was easier to carry off the property? Raped me then taken me? Tristan rid the world of a despicable human being. "Do you think he was working alone?"

"There's no sign that anyone else was with him. But where there's one, there are others. Especially, when money's exchanged." His lips twisted regrettably. "He didn't have ID on him. We'll know more once they run his fingerprints."

"The Frenchman told me it wasn't over," I said, my words a mere whisper.

Tristan squeezed my hand. "That doesn't mean he'd risk coming all the way here to get you."

"He'd just hire someone else who would."

He said nothing, knowing I was right.

"Why won't he just give up? Why won't he just go after someone else?" I gasped. "That sounded awful. I should have never said that."

He brushed his thumb over the back of my hand, likely feeling me tensing up. "I know what you meant. I know you don't want anyone else going through what you've gone through."

I nodded, hating that I'd verbalized what I was feeling in that moment.

"We don't know this guy was connected to the Frenchman," he explained. "And if he was, maybe after this second failed attempt, he'll stop. But I can tell you one thing. Until we know for sure, we're not getting lax when it's your life we're dealing with."

I pulled in a deep breath. I still couldn't believe this was my life. It was amazing I was still holding it together. Was it just a matter of time before I broke down? Was it just a matter of time before I needed heavy meds to sleep? Was it just a matter of time before they got me?

"Stop whatever it is you're thinking right now."

I looked to Tristan who leveled me with serious eyes.

"I'm not gonna let anything happen to you."

I hoped to God he was right.

CHAPTER TWENTY-FIVE
Tristan

When we returned to the dorm, Briggs escorted Kresley up to her room while I parked the car. I didn't want to leave her side, but I wasn't gonna lie. I needed a minute alone to wrap my head around what happened back there.

I just killed someone. And while I knew the guy was a monster, I prayed it wouldn't haunt me. I had enough haunting me.

But what was the alternative?

If I didn't kill him, he would've taken Kresley. And that would have broken me.

I pulled into a parking spot, switched off the engine, and dropped my head to the steering wheel. Was I more upset at myself for missing the signs outside the shelter? Or that I almost lost Kresley? I knew the truth. I knew I couldn't have lived with myself if anything happened to her. As much as I fought us happening, we had happened. And calling it a mistake had been the biggest lie I'd ever told.

I slammed my hands on the steering wheel, hating that I'd need to face Marco *and* Kresley's parents. Sure, I killed the threat. But it didn't mean I hadn't left Kresley in danger because I needed to prove that I didn't have feelings for her. *That* had been my biggest mistake.

I pulled my shit together and stepped out of the car.

Someone shoved my chest, slamming me against the car door and holding me there. I reached for my gun, freezing when I saw it was Marco glaring at me.

"Explain," he growled.

"Let go of me," I ordered.

He released me, but his eyes never left mine.

"There's nothing to explain. Somehow, the fucker bypassed the security we had in place. I saw him running through the woods toward her. I alerted her. Then shot him in the back."

His eyes narrowed. "You shot him in the back? Why weren't you right next to her?"

"She didn't want me with her, so I was giving her some space."

"I don't give a fuck what she wants. We do what's best for her."

I clenched my teeth. I didn't need him telling me I should've been doing what's best for her. I already fucking knew.

"I should've been there," Marco said, seemingly pissed at not only me but at himself.

"You never go to the shelter with us. Besides, this would've happened either way since he somehow bypassed our cameras."

He ran his hands through his hair, looking as tired and angry as he probably felt.

"Go be with your wife. Briggs is here. And I promised I wouldn't leave Kresley's side tonight."

"What's that mean?" he snapped.

"You know what that means."

"For someone who didn't want to take this job, you're fucking acting like it's something more."

"I care about her, Marco. I won't let anything happen to her."

"Like today?" he asked, really testing my patience.

"Fuck you." I was no employee. I was his fucking partner.

Indecision played across his tired eyes.

"Go be with your wife," I repeated. "The guys are following leads back at the office, and she's got two of us here."

"I need to see her," Marco said, fatherly concern coloring his tone.

I sighed. "Yeah, of course."

We arrived at the dorm to find Briggs in a chair outside Kresley's room. He stood when he saw Marco and me approaching.

"How's your wife?" Briggs asked, giving Marco a half-hug pat on the back.

"She and the baby are good. Shouldn't be long now before she delivers the doc says," Marco explained. He nodded toward Kresley's door. "I need a minute." He tapped on Kresley's door. "It's Marco."

Her door opened.

"You okay, ma'am?" he asked her.

She laughed, but it cracked as tears threatened to fall. "Yes."

He walked her into her room and closed the door behind them. Though the rumble of his deep voice carried through the door, he kept his voice low enough that I couldn't hear what he was saying. Was he asking her about us? Was he asking her if I failed her?

I left Briggs in the hall and went to shower, needing to wash off the blood that was still caked under my fingernails from tying him up. I wondered if Kresley had noticed it while she held my hand in the car.

I returned to my room a short time later, slipped into some basketball shorts and a T-shirt, and strapped my gun underneath. I left my room just as Marco stepped out of Kresley's room. I found it difficult to look him in the eyes, not knowing what Kresley had told him.

"Walk me out," he said, without even bothering to look at me.

I glanced to Briggs who sat back in the chair keeping guard.

"You need to be careful," Marco said as we made our way down the stairs.

"What's that mean?"

"This isn't over."

Those words hit me like a punch to the gut. "How can you be sure?"

"No one likes to fail twice," Marco said. "We need both of you on her at all times."

"Agreed."

"She told me she wants you in her room and Briggs outside." He pushed open the front door. I stopped. He turned to face me. "Don't let anything happen to her."

"I won't."

He stared at me for a long time, and I wondered what the hell she said to him. Then he nodded and walked away. "I'll be in touch," he called over his shoulder.

"Take care of your wife."

He raised his fist into the air.

I hurried back inside, taking two stairs at a time, desperate to check on Kresley. "She told Marco she wants you out here and me inside," I told Briggs.

He lifted his brows. "I bet she does."

I cocked my head, pegging him with serious eyes.

"Poor taste?" he asked.

"I'd say."

He stood from the chair and pulled it to the side. "You did good out there today."

"Just doing my job." I knocked on Kresley's door. "It's Tristan."

The door opened and Kresley stood there in her pajamas, her hair down and falling over her shoulders, and her eyes still red from crying. She'd never looked more beautiful. She stepped back and I followed her in, closing the door and locking it. She turned to me and walked right into my arms, burying her head beneath my chin as I held her to me. She felt so small. So fragile. So…mine.

"You okay?" I asked, breathing in the fruity scent of her hair, such a welcome scent after such a horrific day.

"I am now."

"Come on. I wanna hold you," I said.

She slipped her hand into mine and walked me to her bed.

"Hold on." I released her hand and moved to the corner of the room. I reached up and pointed the camera toward the ceiling. Then, I grabbed the desk chair and forced the back of it under the doorknob for added security. I switched on the small lights hanging around the walls before switching off the main light.

We both climbed under the covers. I wrapped my arms around her and pulled her to my chest. We lay there for a long time, just breathing each other in. I wondered what ran through her mind. And though I didn't want to push her, I didn't want her to feel alone. "You wanna talk about it?" I asked.

"Yeah."

I held my breath, preparing myself for whatever came out of her mouth.

"I wanna know if you're really okay," she said.

"I wanna know if *you're* really okay."

She lifted her head so she could look me in the eyes. "I asked you first."

I was the bodyguard. I didn't need her worrying about me. "I'm fine."

She breathed a sigh of relief and my heart clenched. She really did worry about me. "I talked to my parents while you were with Marco," she said. "They want me to come home."

"What do you want?" I asked.

"I don't know."

"That's a fair answer."

"Yeah?" she asked, surprised by my response.

"You've just been through another traumatic experience. You're away from home. Away from your parents. It's normal to be unsure."

"Would you still be on my security team if I go home?" she asked.

"I don't know. That would depend on what you being home would entail. Your parents have their own security."

She closed her eyes and nodded.

"What?" I asked, not wanting her to make the wrong decision because of me.

"I don't want those people to dictate what I do. I want my degree. And I'm so close. But I also don't want my parents to worry. And, I don't want to constantly be looking over my shoulder knowing at any time what happened today could happen again, and I might be alone."

I lifted my hand to her cheek, brushing strands of hair away from her face. "You will never be alone again."

"I don't know if that's reassuring or creepy."

Our quiet laughter was the only sound in her silent room.

"I wish I could tell you what to do, but it's your decision to make. If you go home, you'll be more contained. Here, you're out in the open, whether we secure areas or not."

"Are you trying to make me go home?" she asked.

"I just want you to do what makes you feel safest."

"I feel safest when I'm with you."

I closed my eyes. How could she say that after I almost let him get to her? The events of the day weighed heavily on my mind. Seeing the guy running into the woods. The gunshot. Seeing Kresley go down. Her trembling body when I pulled her up.

"Stop whatever you're thinking right now," she said.

I opened my eyes and stared into her pretty blue ones. "That's my line."

She grinned. "I like your lines."

I brushed my thumb over her cheek, so soft and delicate—so Kresley even when she was being tough.

"As long as they're not lines meant to push *me* away," she amended.

I found it difficult to hold her gaze, but I forced myself to. Forced myself to be honest with her. "I want to see what this is," I admitted, knowing I never should have let it get this far. But it had. And there wasn't a damn thing I could do about it now. I was in too deep. We both were. "I was wrong to push you away. That was about me and not you."

Her heartbeat accelerated, and I could feel it against my chest.

"That makes you happy?" I asked.

"Yes."

"You might find that you don't even like me once you get to know me better," I said.

"I know you."

I scoffed.

"Well, since we're being honest—"

"Uh oh," I said. "Should I be scared?"

She nodded. "That girl at the bar…?"

"Was just some girl who planted her ass next to me. I was there to watch you."

"It was your night off."

I rolled my eyes. "There's no night off when it's your safety. And full disclosure. I wanted to hurt any guy who got near you."

"Like Chris?"

"Fucking Chris needs to stay away from my girl."

Her eyes widened and I loved that my words affected her like that.

A brief silence passed between us and I could see her wheels at work. "Will you tell me what makes you cry out in your sleep?"

Fuuuuck.

I knew my dreams would come up, and I really wanted to come clean to her. But I didn't feel comfortable laying it all on the table when she'd just been through hell. This night was about making *her* feel better. Making *her* feel safe. Not about me and my fucked up dream. "I must've been having a nightmare," I said, hoping that would be enough of an answer to appease her for the time being.

"That didn't sound like a one-time nightmare. That sounded like something that happens often. Something that you were remembering."

Dammit.

I looked away from her expectant eyes. She'd had a shit day and still wanted to know about my demons. But I knew tonight wasn't the time to unload all my baggage on her.

"You don't have to tell me," she finally said. "But know I'm here when you're ready."

I met her gaze. "Tomorrow." I tightened my arms around her. "I just really need to kiss you right now."

Her lips curved up in the corners. "And I just really need you to."

I leaned forward and pressed my lips to hers. They were minty and soft, and I knew we both needed to get lost in this kiss until everything else disappeared into a distant memory. This kiss wasn't meant to lead to sex. That was the furthest thing from my mind tonight. We both needed to feel safe. To feel like we were home. And having Kresley in my arms was definitely beginning to feel like home for me. The only home I've had in a long fucking time.

I pulled away first. "You know this goes against everything I teach new recruits."

"Kissing the client?"

"Falling for the client," I admitted.

I watched her swallow down hard and realized that she hadn't seen that coming.

"I plan everything," I explained. "I think things through. I consider multiple outcomes to every situation in order to do my job well. But *you*. You walked into my life and made those things impossible."

"Are you looking for an apology?" she asked.

I shook my head. "I just want you to know the truth. I know you like when I'm honest with you."

"Will you be able to protect me if we…"

"Take this further?" I asked.

She nodded.

I dragged my teeth over my bottom lip, searching for the right answer—the *honest* answer. "I'd like to say yes.

I'd like to tell you that being important to me makes me protect you better. But honestly? I'm not sure."

"Because I'm a distraction?"

"You deserve my undivided attention when we're together. But, to protect you, your surroundings are what require my undivided attention. So, I'm not sure how to do both."

The disappointment in her eyes nearly leveled me. I wasn't trying to hurt her. But everything out of my mouth just kept doing that. "So, what does that mean?" she asked.

"It means we need to figure out how I can do both."

A small smile tipped her lips.

And knowing she could still smile, after everything she'd just been through, told me she was it for me.

CHAPTER TWENTY-SIX
Kresley

I woke up the next morning to Tristan's arms wrapped around me and soft kisses to the back of my shoulder. I kept my eyes closed, enjoying the fact that Tristan wasn't bolting out of my room this time. Instead, he was showing me how he felt about being with me.

"I know you're awake," he said, his voice all raspy and sexy.

"I didn't want you to stop what you were doing."

He didn't, only moving his lips to the nape of my neck and kissing me there.

"I could get used to waking up like this," I said.

"How are you feeling?" he asked.

"I'm okay. I slept."

"You were up a lot," he countered.

"But as soon as I felt your arms, I knew I was safe and fell back to sleep."

He tightened his arms around me, and it was the most amazing feeling in the world.

"Did you sleep?" I asked.

"I don't sleep much," he admitted.

"By choice?"

His lips stopped moving. "Not really."

"The nightmare?" I said.

"We're going right for the deep stuff, huh?" he said.

"I want to know you, Tristan. Not just what you decide I get to know. What I deserve to know because I care about you. I know it's why you tried to push me away before. I don't care that you have nightmares. That doesn't make you weak. I just want to know what I can do to help you."

He remained quiet, and I wondered if I'd pushed him too far.

I spun around in his arms and looked him in his eyes. They were so tired, and I knew he hadn't slept at all. "Did you hear me, Tristan? I want to help you because I care about you."

"I heard you."

"*So?*"

"I care about you too," he said.

I smiled, and despite the previous day, it felt good to smile at him. "I wasn't looking for affirmation." I lifted a hand and cupped his cheek, the day-old stubble bristly beneath my hand. "I was looking for you to tell me the truth about your dreams."

"You're not gonna let this go, huh?"

I shook my head.

He avoided my eyes, and I could sense he was weighing his options. Tell me and he'd be vulnerable. Don't tell me and I'd be hurt. "I grew up rich."

My mouth parted, but I closed it quickly because I wanted him to keep talking.

"My parents owned a tech company that made a necessary part for the bigger companies."

I stayed quiet, needing to hear where his story was going.

"We lived in a gated community. You'd think security would be tight, but not that day." A far-off look clouded his eyes, as if he was seeing the day play out in his mind's eye. "I was nine and some men broke into our house. They must've thought my parents were at this big tech convention since all the big wigs were in town for it. But my mom had been feeling sick that day. I remember her asking my dad if she could stay home. He hated to go anywhere without her, so he said he'd stay home too. She didn't want that, but he insisted, saying he hated all those tech geeks." A soft chuckle slipped past Tristan's lips. "She responded by telling him he was the biggest tech geek out there."

I forced a smile that didn't reach my eyes, fearing what he was about to tell me.

"The men showed up in broad daylight. We didn't have the security that's available today, so they were able to sneak in and grab me while I was playing in the game room. I screamed and tried to fight them, but they were stronger than me. My father came barging in with a gun, and I'd never been more relieved in my entire life. I just knew he was going to save the day like my favorite superheroes. The problem was, he didn't really know how to use a gun. He tried to fire it, but the safety was still on. The men wasted no time, shooting him dead."

A sharp breath caught in my throat.

"My mom heard the gunfire and ran in. They turned their guns on her and shot her too."

"Oh, Tristan."

"When the men realized two dead people weren't going to pay them ransom, they fled the scene. And do you know what I did?" He stared at me, awaiting my reply.

For once, I didn't have one.

"Nothing," he said. "I did absolutely nothing."

"You were nine," I said, reeling from the heartbreaking story he shared.

"But I should have done *something*."

"You were *nine*," I repeated. "You were in shock."

He closed his eyes, pained by the recollection of that day.

I hoped to God tears didn't glaze his eyes when they reopened, because all I could see in that moment was Tristan at nine, terrified and alone with his dead parents on the floor in front of him. My stomach clenched, unsure how I would ever look at him the same way again. "I'm so sorry you lost your parents. That is not something anyone should have to endure, especially at nine years old," I said softly.

He nodded and his eyes finally opened, devoid of tears.

"I can't even begin to imagine your nightmares."

"Night-*mare*. The same one every night. Me frozen to the floor while my parents are murdered."

I wrapped my arms around him and held on, tucking my head beneath his chin. I didn't know if I was doing it for his benefit or if I needed the comfort too. It wasn't fair he'd lost his parents in such a horrific way. It wasn't fair he relived that day every time he slept. It wasn't fair that he felt like he was to blame. It wasn't fair that he had to endure any of this alone.

"That's why you wanted me to learn how to shoot a gun," I said, realizing he didn't want what happened to his father to happen to me.

He nodded.

A long stretch of silence passed between us. So many thoughts raced through my brain mixed with so much sympathy for nine-year-old Tristan—*and* twenty-five-year-old Tristan. "Who did you live with after?"

"My grandfather for a short time. When he realized I wasn't dealing well with their deaths, he shipped me off to military school."

I swallowed, realizing it's where he likely developed his tough façade. "Did you get counseling?"

He scoffed. "There's no such thing as counseling at military school. You don't show emotions. You don't talk about emotions. You fall in line or you suffer the consequences."

"*Tristan.* That's why you have the dream. You've never dealt with what happened."

"I assure you, I deal with it every fucking time I close my eyes."

"I have a counselor back home—"

"No shrinks."

"Then, let me be the one who stops your nightmare."

He tightened his arms around me. "I want you to be the one to stop it."

His words shouldn't have been breaking my heart, but they were. He was still that lost little boy, but he was locked in the body of a man.

"You said I was a superhero. But I never claimed to be one. I screw up. I say stupid things. I think I can handle everything on my own…until I can't."

"You've got me now."

He nodded.

"Your parents were the two people shot under your watch." It wasn't a question, more like a realization.

"I'll never be convinced that I couldn't have done something."

"Is that why you became a bodyguard?" I asked.

"It's fucked up, right?"

I shook my head. "If it's what you need to do, then I think it's what you should be doing. And, you're damn good at it."

A long stretch of silence passed between us. I wondered what he was thinking about because my mind was whirling with all he'd told me. It definitely explained a lot about him. His initial anger with me for being what he considered careless. He'd lost the two people he loved most in this world within seconds in their own home. Anything could happen while I was out at a crowded place. It wasn't like his fears were unfounded. He had reason to worry. "I wanna take you home," he said, breaking the silence.

"Where do you live?" I asked.

I could hear the smile in his words. "Not to my home. To yours. To see your parents."

"Oh."

He pulled back so he could look at me. "Don't you want to see them?"

"Of course. I'm just scared they won't let me leave."

His eyes riveted between mine. "Does that mean you plan on staying here?" he asked.

"I think it's my only option."

He rolled me onto my back and settled between my legs, his face hovering over mine. "I am so incredibly proud of you."

"Why?"

"Yesterday was a shit show. And you could've crawled into a ball and lost it. But, look at you. You bounced back like a champ."

I lowered my gaze, embarrassed by his compliment.

"Kresley, you're one of the bravest people I know."

I looked to him and rolled my eyes. "You work with a slew of meatheads packin' heat. *They're* brave."

"Did you really just say packin' heat?"

I nodded. "And I called them meatheads."

"Yeah, I caught that."

I stared into his eyes, scared of all the feelings rushing through me. Though my heart broke for his losses, I knew him now. And I wanted him in so many ways. "Are you going to let me tell my parents about us?"

His head dropped back. "*Fuuuuuck.*"

I laughed, not realizing how much I needed to laugh until it was taking over my entire body.

Tristan looked back down at me, smiling at my uncontrollable laughter. "What's so funny?"

"You."

His brows shot up. "Oh, yeah?"

I nodded. "And good looking."

He laughed. "Is that all you like about me?"

My laughter subsided, and I shook my head. "I like that you make me feel."

"Feel what?"

"Everything."

CHAPTER TWENTY-SEVEN
Tristan

Kresley's parents had come to the office to meet and interview Marco and me before they hired us, so I hadn't been to their home before. But when we pulled up to the elaborate gate and a security guard came out of a security booth, it hit me how freaking rich Kresley was.

She leaned across me to look out my open window to speak to the guard. "Hey, Murphy!"

His face lit up. "Hello, Miss Hastings. So good to have you home."

"It's nice to be home. Just so you know, the car behind us is with us."

"I'm still going to need to check it," he said with an apologetic smile.

She nodded. "Of course."

He returned to his booth and opened the gate for us. As I drove through, I glanced in the rearview mirror and noticed Murphy standing in front of the gate so Briggs couldn't pass until he'd checked him. They weren't taking any risks on the property when it came to security.

A stretch of trees concealed Kresley's house which couldn't be seen from the security booth. We drove up the winding driveway bordered by impeccable landscaping. "This is…"

"Obnoxious?" Kresley asked.

"Safe."

She glanced to me. I hoped the sympathy she'd been showing me since I spewed all my shit earlier would soon disappear from her pretty eyes. I didn't need her pity. I just needed her.

The driveway soon opened up to a circular brick expanse with a huge fountain in the center. Beyond the fountain was a massive Mediterranean style villa. I took it all in, trying to visualize Kresley growing up there. Did she stubbornly jump in the fountain because she was told not to? Did she weave in and out of the arched walkways while being chased by a nanny?

Her parents rushed out the front door as soon as I pulled to a stop, hurrying over to Kresley's door.

"Here goes nothing," she said, before pushing open her door and getting out.

I stepped out but stayed on my side of the car, not really sure what I was supposed to do. I wasn't exactly her guest.

Her parents sandwiched her in a hug. It was understandable, given she was their little girl. And, less than twenty-four hours before, she'd almost been attacked.

"You're crushing me," she said.

They laughed as they released her, stepping back and taking her in, visibly relieved she was standing in front of them in one piece.

Mr. Hastings noticed me standing there. An intimidating glint flashed in his eyes.

Oh, fuck.

He rounded the car and stalked toward me.

I swallowed my nerves, knowing I wanted to be with Kresley, so I'd take whatever he planned to say or do.

He reached out his hand. "Thank you for protecting our daughter."

I shook his hand. "I swore I'd keep her safe."

Kresley's mom hurried over to me and wrapped her arms around me. I didn't know what to do with my hands so I kept them at my sides as the scent of expensive perfume wrapped itself around me. I caught sight of Kresley stifling a smile. "Thank you for keeping her safe."

"Always," I said as she finally released me.

As the Hastings turned and walked toward the front door, I looked to Kresley for a sign of what I should do. Did I wait outside or accompany her inside?

She held up her finger, asking me for some time before she turned and followed her parents inside.

Only then could I finally breathe.

That went better than I expected.

Kresley

I followed my parents down the long hallway lined with family portraits toward the kitchen. I'd told Tristan to hang back so I could talk to my parents in private. I wasn't exactly sure how they were going to take the news that I wasn't staying home—or that I was in a relationship with my bodyguard.

Someone was in the sitting room as we passed by.

"Andre!"

He was standing by the doorway with a big smile on his face.

I rushed over and threw my arms around him. "How are you?"

"Welcome home, Miss Kresley," he said, hugging me back. "I'm fine."

I stepped back and looked at him, taking in the many creases around his eyes and his full head of gray hair. He'd aged in the months since I'd seen him last. "What are you doing here?"

"I'm helping watch over the surveillance monitors," he said with a smile.

"You're *working* here?"

He nodded, looking pleased that he wasn't fired after France.

"I'm so happy to hear that. I miss you."

"I miss you too." He looked at me with sadness in his eyes. "How *are* you?"

"You know me, Andre. I'm tougher than I look."

He forced a smile, and that twinkle I'd seen in his eyes so many times before returned.

"I gotta catch up with my parents. But I'll see you before I leave," I promised him, before moving to the kitchen and slipping onto a stool at the center island. A sense of security swept over me being back home.

My mom stood with the refrigerator door open, gathering an armful of food—a nervous habit when she didn't know what to do or say. My father leaned against the counter with his arms crossed, staring at me like he was seeing a ghost.

"Dad, I'm fine. Stop staring at me like that." I looked to my mom. "And, Mom, stop doing whatever you're doing over there. I'm not hungry. I just want to talk to you guys."

She placed the cheeses and fruit she'd gathered onto the counter and turned to look at me. "Why didn't Stone unpack the car and bring in your belongings?"

"His name is Tristan, and I'm not coming home," I said.

Fear gripped hold of her features. "What?"

My father sighed. "Returning to school is an unnecessary risk."

"We can keep you safe here," my mother promised. "Security is tighter than it's ever been."

"I can't stay locked up forever." I hated that I was hurting them by not agreeing to do what I knew they both wanted me to do.

"Of course you can," my mother said. "You're my baby and I don't want anything to happen to you."

I drew in a deep breath. "I need to finish school and get my degree. I can't let them strip me of that too."

"It's not safe," my father said. "Look what happened yesterday. Who knows what's next."

"But I *was* safe. Tristan protected me," I assured them.

"He won't always be there," my father argued.

I glanced to my mother before looking back to him. "He might be."

My father's eyes jumped from me to my mother then back to me. "What does that mean?"

"I like him, Dad," I explained.

"Well, that's good. Having security you despise wouldn't work at all," he said.

I shook my head. "No, Dad. I *like* him. I want to be with him, and he wants to be with me."

"That can't happen," my father said, shaking his head and not wanting to hear it.

"Why?"

"Your safety needs to be his top priority."

"It is sir," Tristan said.

Everyone turned to Tristan who now stood in the kitchen doorway, filling it as if he belonged in our home. Like he belonged by my side.

"Kresley's my top priority," Tristan assured them as he walked over and stood beside me at the island. "I hope my attentiveness and actions yesterday proved that to you."

My father closed his eyes, pained by the new information we were dropping on him. When he opened them, his accusatory glare was trained on me. "Is this why you want to go back to school? Is this why you won't stay home where it's safe?"

"No," I assured him. "I have a life there. I have friends. I'm safe with everything I do. And I'm months away from graduating."

"Kresley, someone just came after you," my mother argued.

I knew my parents worried about me. Hell, I was worried too. But I couldn't live my life in fear. I had security looking out for me. And, despite what happened yesterday, there was no saying anyone else would be coming for me.

Tristan placed his hand on my shoulder, giving me his assurance that I was doing the right thing, and spoke to my parents. "I care about your daughter and won't let anything happen to her."

"We don't doubt your intent," my mother said to him. "It's the fact that we can't be sure how well you'll do your job if she becomes a distraction for you. She's our only child, and the thought of anything else happening to her keeps us awake at night."

"I understand," Tristan said. "But if I find myself becoming distracted, I'll resign. I'd never do anything to put Kresley in danger. You have my word."

Tristan

"Well, that went well," Kresley said from the passenger seat as we drove back to Remington that night.

"Are you joking?"

She shook her head. "No, they like you. I can tell."

"I've never met the parents after I'd already met the parents."

Kresley laughed. "Well, you did a great job."

An hour into the drive home, I glanced over at Kresley who'd become quiet. Her head rested against the window and her eyes were closed. After her restless sleep last night, I knew it was just a matter of time before she'd crash. I lowered the radio and continued to drive in silence. I noticed a party supply store coming up on my left and hit my blinker, pulling into the parking lot and parking the car. Briggs pulled up next to me, probably wondering what the hell I was doing. I glanced to Kresley who was still asleep and switched off the engine. "I'll be right back," I whispered.

I stepped out, asking Briggs to hang with the car. I was in and out of the store in five minutes, tucking the small bag containing my purchase into the back of the car so Kresley couldn't see what I'd bought.

When we were back on the road, she glanced to me. "You gonna tell me what you needed at a party supply store?" she asked, all raspy and sleepy.

Dammit. I didn't think I woke her. "Nope."

"So, you're gonna keep secrets from me?"

"Maybe."

She shook her head. "Good relationships are based on trust."

"And sex."

She rolled her eyes. "So, you're using me for my body? That's what this is?"

"I'm a body *guard*, baby. It's in the job title."

Her mouth dropped open. "Oh my God."

I laughed "What?"

"You were right. I might not like you the more I get to know you."

"Take that back," I ordered.

"Nope."

"Take it back, Kresley or—"

"Or what? The mean Tristan will rear his ugly head?" she asked.

"Oh, he'll be rearing his head all right."

She groaned. "*Stop*. I'm starting to hate you again."

I laughed, loving that I could tease her and, in turn, I'd be treated to her smile and sassy ways.

When we returned to the dorm, I asked Briggs to wait for her while she showered, and I ducked into her room. She walked in with her wet hair in a knot on the top of her head as I sat on the edge of her bed.

"What are you doing?" she asked, her eyes moving around her room curiously.

"Just waiting for you."

She smiled as she walked over to me. I opened my legs and she stood between my knees, wrapping her arms around me. "I'm so happy today's over."

"Were you worried?"

"A little. I didn't want to let them down too much," she said.

I slipped my arms around her hips. "I think they're happy to know they raised a strong daughter who, when faced with adversity, can handle it."

"Stop lying."

"I'm not. Most rich kids are unequipped to deal with serious stuff because so much has been done for them. I bet your parents are happy to know you're okay on your own."

"I'm not really on my own."

"You took off to France not knowing anyone but your bodyguard. And six months after the attack, you're here. Give yourself some credit."

She nodded, her eyes darting away from mine.

I didn't want her to go to a dark place, so I tightened my arms around her and fell back so she landed on top of me. She giggled, and it was the purest thing I'd heard in a long fucking time.

"Do you like surprises?" I asked.

She smiled and her eyes lit up. "I love surprises."

I rolled out from under her and slipped off the bed. "Wait for it." I turned off all the lights in the room.

"What are you doing?" she asked, watching me curiously.

I moved back onto the bed and turned her so we both lay on our backs with our heads on her pillow.

Her breath hitched as she stared up at her ceiling.

"I brought the stars to you," I said as we gazed up at the glow-in-the-dark stars I'd stuck to the ceiling above her bed. "Nothing's blocking your view in here."

She grabbed my hand and linked her fingers with mine. "I'm sorry for anything mean I've ever said to you. I take it all back."

"I'm no angel," I assured her. "And, anything you've said, I've deserved."

"True."

We both laughed, knowing it was the truth. I could be a real prick sometimes.

"You're gonna make me, huh?" she mused as she stared up at the stars I'd arranged in a circular pattern.

"Make you what?" I asked, confused by her question.

"Fall in love with you."

I swallowed my surprise. I knew she cared about me but wasn't sure she was feeling anything close to what I was feeling for her. I rolled on top of her and settled between her legs, staring down into her pretty eyes. "I hope so."

She smiled and I captured her smile with my lips.

I'd needed to do that all day long, and now, there was nothing stopping us.

CHAPTER TWENTY-EIGHT
Kresley

If I thought I stuck out with my security before the incident in the woods, now I knew for sure I did. Briggs and Tristan walked like two pillars on either side of me across campus. Thankfully, Marco wasn't back yet because there wasn't a doubt in my mind he would've led the way. Thank God for small favors.

We walked into the building toward my first class. Briggs followed me inside the classroom.

"Whoa," I said, turning to stop him.

"I've got orders." He walked right past me and over to my professor.

I walked to my seat and pulled out my laptop, ignoring the fact that he was likely telling my professor why he planned to stay in the class. After he spoke to her, I pretended not to notice him standing in the back of the classroom with his arms crossed for the entire lecture. And, as annoyed as I wanted to be, knowing he was there, while Tristan was in the hallway, gave me a sense of security I otherwise wouldn't have had.

When the professor dismissed class, I gathered my things and headed toward the front door. Tristan and Briggs stood in the hallway. I smiled at Tristan, but his game face was on and he avoided my eyes. Though we needed to keep our relationship quiet, that wasn't the reason for his inattention. He was worried. His eyes were taking in everyone and everything around us. I just wasn't used to seeing him nervous. Did he know something I didn't know? Had they traced the fingerprints back to someone with no ties to the money exchanged?

As we walked across campus, those thoughts plagued my mind. Not the people playing Frisbee. Not the beautiful trees around the quad. Not the students rushing to their next classes.

At dinner, as many times as I tried to meet Tristan's gaze, he dodged my eyes, watching the crowded room instead.

"So?" Elodie said, pulling my attention from Tristan.

"So," I repeated.

"We've got an entourage tonight," Alice acknowledged.

I nodded, stuffing a fork full of pasta into my mouth to save myself the inquisition that was inevitably coming. They knew I'd gone home yesterday, but not why.

"Did something happen that requires two bodyguards at dinner?" Elodie asked, unable to conceal the worry in her eyes.

I glanced from Briggs to Tristan, in different corners of the room. I looked back to Elodie and nodded.

Alice's eyes widened. "Are you okay?"

Elodie's eyes assessed my face. "Did someone hurt you?"

I shook my head as I swallowed down my food.

"But they tried?" Alice asked.

I nodded. "Tristan saved me."

They both spun on their seats to look to Tristan standing on the other side of the room. Still, his eyes were on the room and not on the three of us.

"Hot and brave," Alice said.

"And taken," I added.

They spun back around to face me with their eyes bugging out of their heads.

I stifled a smile while nodding my response to their unasked question.

They squealed, causing the people around us to turn to see what was happening at our table.

"*Shhhhhh.*" I closed my eyes, embarrassed by the unneeded attention.

"I knew it!" Elodie said, completely proud of her foresight.

"Who caved first?" Alice asked.

I thought about her question. They still didn't know we'd slept together and then all hell broke loose. "It was mutual. The more time we spent together…it just happened."

Alice's brows shot up. "It?"

I cocked my head. They didn't know when to quit.

They squealed again.

I dropped my head and shook it, not bothering to mention that wasn't what I meant. Because in the grand scheme of things, *it* had happened too.

They eventually stopped grilling me, and we finished eating dinner. We returned to the dorm a little while later accompanied by Tristan and Briggs. I stopped short when we stepped onto our floor. Marco stood against the wall outside my room. A smile spread across my face as I left the girls at their room and hurried over to him. "Welcome back."

"Welcome back, big guy," Alice called down the hallway.

"How's your wife?" Elodie called.

"Good," Marco grunted, before turning and opening my door so I could step inside.

Tristan and Briggs retreated to their rooms as Marco and I stepped into my room. He pulled out my desk chair and flipped it backward, taking a seat that way. "Sit."

I sat on the edge of my bed. "You're scaring me."

"My wife is scheduled for a C-section in two days, so I'm only here because I need you to know what our guys at the office just found."

My heart began to speed up. "Okay."

"The man in the woods was paid to kidnap you. His name was Juron VanSang, and he was wired half a million dollars to take you, drug you, and get you back to France."

"Okay." I swallowed down the lump of emotion in my throat. "I figured it was something like that."

"Do you have any idea why these men in France are so keen on getting you? It's not making sense anymore. If they wanted a rich kid for ransom, there are plenty out there. Why are they dead set on you?"

I shrugged, just as confused as anyone. "Do you know where in France he was supposed to take me?"

He nodded. "A warehouse outside of Paris. We alerted the authorities there and some of our men are already on their way there to see if they can find anything. We figure VanSang would've had to let the people footing the bill know once he had you. When that call never came, they would've aborted the mission. But that doesn't mean they wouldn't have left any clues. If they did, my guys will find them."

I nodded, struggling to digest the information. "Does Tristan know about this?"

He cocked his head, clearly seeing the look in my eyes that accompanied Tristan's name. "I'm about to fill him in right now. I just got the call and wanted you to hear it from me."

"Thank you for telling me, Marco."

He pushed himself to his feet, towering over me. "We're going to keep you safe, Kresley."

The sound of my name on his lips sent a chill through me. I'd wanted him to call me by my name for so long that now that he had, it scared me. It told me he was worried. And if Marco was worried, I needed to be worried too.

Once he left, I changed into my pajamas and attempted to work on my homework. But my mind was reeling, making homework impossible.

It wasn't like I didn't know VanSang's intent when he appeared in the woods at the shelter. But hearing the actual plan—a plan that had been strategically put in place and paid for—made it that much more real.

This wasn't some game. This was my life.

A little after nine, there was quiet tapping on my door. I slipped off my bed and went to it.

"Kresley," Tristan said.

I opened my door, relieved to see him standing there in his basketball shorts and T-shirt with his holster under it. "Is it okay if I come in?"

I tipped my head to the side. "You're asking now?"

He shrugged. I stepped back and he walked in, moving to my desk and leaning against it.

"I'm not a fragile flower, Tristan." I closed the door. "You don't need to walk on eggshells with me." I walked over and stood in front of him.

"Do you have any idea how hard it is for me to hear what Marco just told me and not want to go out there and hurt any person involved in this?"

I took his hand in mine, knowing he meant what he said. He'd told me he'd been taught not to have feelings while away at military school. So, this had to be all new for him—having feelings for me while worrying about me at the same time. "But I'm okay."

"I know. I just can't stop thinking about what could've happened if he got to you."

My eyes dropped away from his, the thought a terrifying one. What if he had gotten to me?

"What are *you* thinking?"

I glanced up at him, pushing any fears I had aside. "I'm thinking I'm happy my bodyguard gets to sleep in my bed."

His own worries seemed to disappear. "Oh yeah?"

I nodded.

He pushed off the desk and stepped forward, the hunger in his eyes impossible to ignore. I backpedaled, as if it were a game, until my back hit the door. He caged me in and dropped his forehead to mine. "Do you know how hard it is following you around all day without being able to touch you?"

I swallowed down the knot that suddenly jumped to my throat.

He grabbed my ass with both hands and lifted me right off the floor.

I wrapped my legs around his hips and dangled my arms over his shoulders, expecting him to carry me to the bed. But he didn't. He held me against the door and captured my mouth with his. He tipped his head, giving himself the best angle to devour my lips—and he did. His tongue pushed inside, tousling with mine in a slow and steady chase.

He pulled back once we were both good and breathless. "There are so many things I want to do with you, Kresley Hastings."

My brows shot up. "Like?"

"Oh, I think you know."

I laughed.

"But I also wanna take you out."

"Oh yeah?"

He nodded. "What do you say?"

"A date?"

"Yes."

I stifled the giant grin fighting to overtake my face. "Where will we go?"

"Not an Italian restaurant or lame open mic night, that's for sure."

"Someone jealous?" I teased.

"Fucking Chris. He's lucky I didn't hurt him."

I rolled my eyes. "So, how will a date work? Will Briggs have to come with us?"

His eyes pinched tightly for a second. I knew all the details of us trying to go out together would be a frustrating situation for him. "I have no fucking idea how it's gonna work," he admitted. "All I know is the guys will never let me live it down that I was the one to break rule number one."

"Who cares," I said. "You ended up with the girl."

He smiled. "I did, didn't I?"

CHAPTER TWENTY-NINE
Tristan

I paced the floor in Marco's room as sunlight was just beginning to push through the blinds. "We'll meet you downstairs at the car," I informed Briggs who sat on Marco's bed, still looking half asleep. "You are not to chime in on our conversation or give us any looks or I'll use my weapon on you."

Briggs held up his hands in surrender. "Dude, I'm not saying anything."

"And you're to hang back. Promise me you'll stay with the car. I'm obviously armed and I've already secured the location."

"Yes. For the tenth time, I've got it," Briggs said.

I nodded, pulling in a deep breath before walking to the door. "Get to the car. We'll be down in five minutes."

"Yes, sir," Briggs said.

I flipped him the bird and walked out of the room, more nervous for this date than I'd expected to be. It's not like Kresley and I hadn't spent time alone together. It was more about everyone else butting into our business.

This definitely wasn't easy for me. I was going from her bodyguard to someone who needed security while with her. It was going to be a slippery slope to maneuver. And, if I wanted to be with her, I'd have to endure the jests as well as my own anxiety about it.

I stopped in front of her door, checked my jeans and collared navy shirt, then knocked. When I heard her feet shuffle inside, I said, "It's me."

She opened the door and my eyes widened.

Holy shit.

She glanced down at her green dress. "Am I overdressed?"

I thought the red dress she wore on her date with the tool was hot. But this short strapless sundress was in a league of its own. "God, no. You look gorgeous."

She smiled.

I stepped forward and cupped her cheeks, dropping a kiss to her forehead. "I know better than to smudge a girl's lip gloss."

"Oh, yeah? How do you know that?"

I pulled back, my nerves buzzing to life. "Oh…I…"

She placed her small hand on my chest, patting it gently. "I'm joking. I'm sure you've had plenty of girlfriends."

I wouldn't call any of them girlfriends. Time-fillers maybe. But not girlfriends.

"What?" she asked, clearly reading the look on my face.

I shook off her question. "Let's head out. The car's out front."

Since it was not even nine yet, the floor was eerily quiet as we stepped into the empty hallway.

"Have *fuuuuun,*" Elodie and Alice sang from their open door down the hallway.

I spoke too soon.

Kresley laughed and I ignored them.

"Go get him, girl!" Alice called likely waking the whole damn floor.

Kresley snorted as we walked in the opposite direction of her nosey friends toward the stairwell.

"I knew you'd cave, bodyguard!" Elodie called.

I placed one hand on the small of Kresley's back to guide her into the stairwell and held my free hand over my head, flipping them off.

Alice and Elodie cracked up.

"Tell me you didn't flip them off," Kresley said.

When I didn't answer, she rolled her eyes knowing I definitely had.

We took the stairs to the first floor. "You've gotta admit they remind you of Velma and Daphne," I said.

She turned and looked at me. "I knew I wasn't the only one."

We laughed as we stepped outside.

The car was parked by the sidewalk, and Briggs waited by the back door like a chauffeur.

"Son of a bitch," I mumbled.

"What?" Kresley asked.

"Good morning, Miss Hastings," Briggs said as he opened the back door. He glanced to me. "Sir."

"Would you knock it off?" I shoved him toward the front seat and helped Kresley into the backseat, following her in and closing the door. It felt weird to sit in the back with her, but I willed my nerves to settle the hell down and enjoy the day.

"Would you care for any particular music?" Briggs asked from the driver's seat as he looked at us through the rearview mirror.

Kresley placed her hand on my thigh, clearly trying to ease my nerves. "Anything's fine," she answered.

He nodded then pulled away from the sidewalk and drove us through town.

My knee bounced anxiously as silence filled the car. I couldn't risk speaking to Kresley for fear of Briggs using whatever I said against me later. Kresley squeezed my thigh, presumably trying to relax me and assure me this was a good idea when everything inside me was telling me it wasn't.

Briggs hit his blinker and took the ramp onto the highway just as the radio switched on.

I breathed a small sigh of relief knowing we'd get at our destination soon. And, we'd be alone.

Kresley leaned into me and whispered, "Where are we going?"

"It's a surprise."

"If I guess, will you tell me?"

"No."

She pouted, which ordinarily would've come off childish, but on her it was funny since I knew she always wanted to know everything.

"I'll give you a hint," I offered.

Her face lit up and her blue eyes rounded, so childlike and happy. After all she'd been through, it meant a lot to see her happy—and know I had something to do with it. I just hoped my surprise was worthy of her excitement.

"It's revolves around two things you love."

Her lips twisted as she considered what I now realized came out like a riddle. "Two things I love. *Hmmmm.*"

I smiled, pleased with myself that I could give her this…even just temporarily.

She linked our fingers and didn't try to fill the silence with small talk. I loved that about her. She could read me. She knew I was uncomfortable and wasn't pushing me to come out of my shell in front of Briggs. *Though*, if I clammed up on our date, it would be a different story.

Briggs took the exit a short while later bringing us closer to our destination.

Kresley gazed out her window, clearly noticing the ocean in the distance. She peeked at me and lifted her brows in question.

I shrugged, all the answer she was getting.

We drove a little further before we pulled into a marina parking lot.

Her eyes jumped from me to the marina lined with boats. "Are we going on a boat?"

"Maybe."

She smiled.

Most college girls would've been blown away by the notion of a boat ride for a first date. But I knew for Kresley it was no big deal because her father owned a yacht. But her eyes still lit up like this was an amazing surprise. I loved that she never acted like a billionaire's daughter. I also loved that this wasn't the surprise.

Briggs cut the engine.

"Wait here for a second," I said to Kresley.

She nodded, knowing we had protocols, especially now.

I stepped out and spoke to Briggs who'd joined me outside with the bag I'd packed over his shoulder. "Bring the bag to the boat and double-check that Roger's the captain. Then sweep the boat for bugs and explosives."

"You sure you don't want me on there with you?" he asked.

"I've got it covered."

"If you're not back by sundown, I'm coming with backup," he assured me.

"It'll be fine," I assured him.

He nodded then took off for the boat.

I walked over to Kresley's door and opened it, holding my hand out for her. "Sorry about that."

She grasped my hand and let me pull her out. The sun was not quite overhead, given it wasn't even ten, but there wasn't a cloud in the sky. "Should I have brought my bathing suit?"

"Maybe next time," I said, walking her toward the boats.

"There's gonna be a next time?" she asked, totally fishing for assurances.

"I guess we'll have to see how this date goes."

She playfully bumped me with her hip, sending me off balance.

I laughed, following Briggs who checked the area around us, while I did the same. We made our way down Pier C until we stood at the end.

Kresley's eyes moved over the sixty-foot yacht in front of us. "Are we going on this one?"

I nodded, watching for her reaction.

"It's beautiful."

"I worked security on it last summer. The owner got into a lot of trouble and owed me a favor…or ten."

She laughed.

"He lent me his boat and his captain."

"Tristan, that you?" Roger called out from the captain's chair on the top level. He wore a white captain's hat that had seen better days. But it fit the whole drunken captain persona he had going on.

"How's it going, Captain?" I called up.

"Well, the dick isn't sailing today and you are, so I'd say it's a step in the right direction."

I laughed. "Yeah, well that dick gave me the boat for the day. So, I'm going to have to refrain from insulting him."

Roger swatted his hand at the air. "Who's this beauty you've got with you?"

"This is Kresley."

Roger stood, removed his hat, and bowed to her, totally overdoing it. But drunken sea captain's loved beautiful women. And Kresley was definitely a beautiful woman. "Pleased to make your acquaintance," he said.

Kresley curtsied, totally playing along. "The pleasure is all mine, Captain."

"I like her," Roger said with a bounce to his brows as he returned his hat to his head. "Alrighty. Stop lollygagging and get aboard so we can set sail."

I helped Kresley aboard and jumped on after. We moved to the back to a white leather sofa seat which seemed like the best place to take in the beautiful Saturday morning.

"Two things I love?" she asked, her brows raised in question as the boat purred to life.

"The ocean," I explained.

"That's only one," she said, still trying to figure out my cryptic clue.

I draped my arm around her shoulders and pulled her into my side. "You'll find out soon."

She slipped off her shoes and tucked her legs up under her, relaxing into me. "Thank you, Tristan."

I didn't say anything, hoping if she liked this so much, she'd love the real surprise.

Kresley

He'd taken me on a boat. I hated that he felt like he needed to do something extravagant for our first date. I would've been happy getting takeout and watching a movie—as long as he was with me. I thought he understood that. But he'd gone to great lengths to make this day happen, so I'd never let on that I didn't need all this.

"Where'd you grow up?" I asked as the captain pulled out into open waters.

"Not too far from you in Monterey."

"Where was your military school?"

"Alturas."

"Did they have sports and stuff like other schools?" I asked, curious about what it was like.

He nodded.

"I bet you played football."

He smirked. "Running back."

"I would've loved to see you play. I loved high school football games."

"Don't tell me you were a cheerleader."

I shook my head. "Just a fan. What do you think it would've been like if we met back then?" I asked.

"I would've thought you were hot."

I rolled my eyes.

"Then I would've tried to get your best friend's number just to piss you off."

"You're such a jerk."

He shrugged.

"So, why piss me off?" I asked. "Why not just ask for my number?"

"Come on, Kres. We both know you would've turned me down."

He was right. Any guy forward enough to ask for my number from the get-go didn't seem serious. They seemed like players who asked for every girl's number. "I like that you know me."

He smiled and when he smiled like that—like he could really see me, I wanted to melt into a big puddle of useless goo.

"I like when you let down your guard," I said.

"Yeah, well, that could get us both into a lot of trouble," he explained.

"Is that why we're out here? Less chance of trouble if you let down your guard?"

"I told you why we're out here. You love the ocean. Not to mention, you're safe."

I pulled back and assessed his face, trying to figure out what I was missing. "Am I still waiting for the second thing?"

"It's not obvious?" he asked.

I shook my head.

He took that as his opportunity, capturing my lips and kissing me slow and purposeful. I never imagined kissing Tristan would have the ability to conjure up so many emotions inside of me. But it did. And I couldn't imagine ever getting sick of doing it.

He pulled back with a smile. "I really like you."

I smiled, incapable of not in that moment. I met him halfway, kissing him and taking the lead, showing him how much his words meant to me. Since we met, he shared very few personal thoughts, so anything he shared just helped me to understand who the real Tristan Stone was.

"Anyone need a drink?" Captain shouted down to us.

We pulled apart, both grinning like fools.

"You want anything?" Tristan asked me.

I shook my head.

"We're all good," he shouted up to him.

"I could see that," Captain called down.

I settled back into Tristan's side, taking in the ocean on all sides of us. The blue water always took my breath away regardless of the number of times I sailed. Having Tristan by my side made it extra special this time. The smell of the ocean mixed with the heat of the sun beating down, the mist from the water shooting up, and Tristan's strong arm around me made it all feel like home. "Are we dropping anchor out here?" I asked.

Tristan smirked. "You'll see."

And I did see a short time later. A small island appeared in the distance. It didn't look like it housed a resort, but a small beach bordered one side while the rest of the small isle was filled with lush green vegetation. My mouth formed an O. He didn't? My head whipped around to see Tristan's smiling face.

"It's ours for the day," he explained.

"You *rented* an island?"

"I told you my parents were wealthy. I have more money than I know what to do with in the bank. They would want me to use it for a good reason."

"*Tristan.*" I didn't want to make him feel bad for giving me something I wanted, but it was way too much.

"*Kresley,*" he mimicked.

I stared out at the island as we neared it. "This is…"

"Just say you love it and let's be done with this conversation."

"I love it. It's beyond thoughtful." I looked back to him. "But after today, I don't want you spending money on me. I'm very low maintenance."

He smirked. "I seem to recall that same word getting us to where we are right now."

I tipped my head to the side. "So, you wouldn't take it back?"

"It made you hate me, didn't it?"

"You wanted me to hate you?" I asked

"I *needed* you to hate me. This is a lot more complicated. Hate is concrete. This…" He motioned between us with his hand. "This wasn't supposed to happen."

"Do you regret it?"

"I regret a lot of things, but falling for you is not one of them."

I lifted my hand to his cheek, cupping it gently. "You've fallen for me?"

He stared into my eyes. "Hard."

Ripples rolled through my belly as the boat hit a few choppy waves, jerking us forward and back. I didn't mind. Tristan just tightened his arm around me. Being alone out there on the ocean with Tristan was all I needed. And all I wanted. It was my fairy tale come to life.

As we came upon the dock jutting out of the island, Captain slowed the boat and pulled us to a stop next to it.

Tristan stood, taking my hand and pulling me up and into his chest. He wrapped his arms around me and stared down into my eyes. "Just you, me, and the birds out here. Even Captain Roger has strict orders to stay on the boat."

My brows shot up. "Oh yeah?"

He nodded before releasing me and reaching under the seat we'd been sitting on. He grabbed the bag tucked underneath and slung it over his shoulder. "So, tell me." He linked our hands again. "What do you plan to do on your private island?"

"I'm sure I could think of a few things."

He pulled me toward the steps and we disembarked onto the dock.

"No one lives here?" I asked.

He shook his head. "It's for sale, but they've been renting it out in the meantime. Without a place to stay, most people just use it for day trips or camping."

"Camping sounds nice."

"I did not take you for a camping kind of girl."

"Okay, so maybe I don't want to be in the middle of the woods with all those bugs," I admitted. "But camping out under the stars on a beach would be a dream come true."

"We could do that sometime."

"But not tonight?" I asked.

He shook his head regrettably. "We only have until sundown before Briggs threatened to send the cavalry looking for us."

I said nothing, hating that I was this fragile flower that everyone needed to protect. Would anyone ever view me as strong? Would I ever be allowed to stand on my own two feet?

He reached over and took my chin with his fingers. "But Briggs knew how much I wanted to do this for you, so he agreed to help."

"Marco would kick your ass if he knew."

"He's not here, is he?"

I laughed as we followed a path through some trees to the beach. As soon as we reached it, I slipped off my shoes and walked barefoot, letting the warm sand seep between my toes.

Tristan grabbed a blanket from his bag and spread it out on the sand. Before he could do anything else, I reached behind my back and pulled the zipper down on my dress. The light material fell to my feet and I stood there in a black strapless bra and matching panties.

His Adam's apple bobbed as he swallowed down, clearly not expecting my boldness.

"Your turn."

He smirked, clearly not about to be outdone. He grabbed his shirt behind his neck and pulled it off. His shoulder holster cut around the muscles beneath his white tank top like a second skin. He removed it, guns and all, and lay it in the bag he'd brought. Then pulled off the shirt.

I drank him in, never tiring of the perfect view.

He reached for the button on his jeans, slipped it through the slot, then shed his jeans, leaving him in his boxers with that perfect V disappearing beneath the waistband.

He stared me down, the corners of his lips twitching as he awaited my next move.

I took off for the water, running right in and laughing as the cool water engulfed my body. I closed my eyes and spread my arms, spinning around.

No security.

No threat.

No judgment.

Just the two of us alone on an island. I'd never felt more free.

I heard Tristan splashing when he walked into the water. Soon his arms slipped around me and I opened my eyes.

"I love seeing you like this," he said, his blue eyes mirroring the water at our waists.

I slipped my arms over his shoulders. "I feel so free out here."

"I wish you always felt that way."

I tunneled my fingers through the back of his hair, drawing his mouth closer to mine. "I do when I'm with you."

Our lips met in a rush of tongues and teeth. Tristan lifted me off my feet. I linked my ankles behind his back and held on as he walked us deeper into the water with his mouth ravaging mine.

This was what feeling safe in someone's arms felt like. And, if I was dreaming, I never wanted to wake up.

Tristan pulled back once our heads were the only parts of us above water.

"Don't put me down," I said.

"Why not?"

"I've never…you know…in the ocean."

His brows shot up. "And you want to…you know…in the ocean?"

I nodded as I reached behind my back and unhooked my bra. "I'm gonna need some help." I reached down and tried to shimmy out of my panties while still in his grip. He somehow managed to pull them down the rest of the way without dropping me. Once I was naked, he wasted no time, shoving down his boxers. Our chests heaved as we stared into each other's eyes. He lifted his hand and cupped my cheek. I leaned into it. "I love how you constantly surprise me. Because just when I think I know you, you always do something that keeps me on my toes."

"And?"

"And I like it," he said.

I could feel his erection pressing between my thighs. So could he. "I don't have a condom," he explained.

"I'm on the pill."

"Are you sure?"

"Yes."

"Well, know I've been tested."

I nodded, wanting nothing more than to feel every inch of him inside of me. Anxiousness fluttered in my chest as I shifted my hips, rubbing against him. Our eyes stayed locked and I'd never felt more vulnerable. But there was something about our connection that gave me confidence. That filled me with want and need. That urged me on.

"Keep looking at me like that," he said.

"Like how?"

"Like you see me."

"I do see you, Tristan. And I love what I see."

He kept his eyes on mine as he thrust up at the same time that I sank down. I thought sex in water would be slippery and awkward, but we managed it on the first try. I closed my eyes, reveling in the feel of him stretching me wide. The water mixed with his bare skin was almost too much. But I wanted to see his face. I opened my eyes, daring him to keep his on mine. I rocked my hips as he thrust up. I'd never been this exposed with someone before, and I wondered if it was because we knew each other's demons that made us so open. My head dropped back as I fought to keep my eyes on Tristan's. They were hooded but seared into my soul as if he truly did know everything about me and it didn't change the way he felt. "Oh, my God, Tristan." I felt him everywhere as I rode him.

"I'm right with you, baby," he gritted out.

My hips kept moving and he kept thrusting. Before long, everything between my thighs tightened. I held my breath and my eyes pinched tight as tingles erupted, rippling out to my fingertips and toes as Tristan kept pumping his hips. I opened my eyes and his were closed. It gave me a minute to appreciate the ecstasy on his face before he dropped his face into my shoulder, groaning until his hips finally stilled.

We both gasped for breath as we held each other, still connected and reeling from some amazing ocean sex.

He finally lifted his head and looked me in the eyes. "Totally surprised."

I laughed, before pressing my lips to his.

He carried me back to the beach a little while later and placed me down on the blanket. I grabbed his T-shirt and slipped it on while he pulled on his jeans. He sat down beside me and wrapped his arm around me, pulling me into his chest. We enjoyed each other as well as the sun, just taking in the stretch of ocean surrounding us. I'd never been happier. No one was coming out of the water. No one could catch us by surprise. I was safe and the notion released the heaviness that had been sitting on my chest like a weight since France.

That's why this had been my fairy tale. I knew I'd only ever be free if there was no possibility of a threat. And out there, surrounded by nothing but water, there wasn't.

A little while later, Tristan reached into the bag and pulled out two sandwiches and drinks. We ate in silence watching the ocean waves in front of us. No boats came into sight. No helicopters or planes flew overhead. It really was our very own deserted island.

"Tell me about your last girlfriend," I said, suddenly wanting to know everything about him.

He glanced to me with apprehension etched in his features.

"That bad?"

He shook his head. "I've never had a girlfriend."

My brows knit together. "What? Why?"

He shrugged, but I knew there was more to it.

"But you've had sex."

He rolled his eyes. "Obviously."

"So, why not date anyone?"

"Girls are too much trouble."

I bumped him with my shoulder. "You mean we're high maintenance and desperate?"

"Exactly."

"I call bullshit," I said, not giving him a chance to dispute it as I climbed onto his lap and straddled him. "You don't like getting close to people. And by having a girlfriend, it means you need to drop the façade and be real with someone. And, girls like to talk. Girls like to get to know the guy they're dating. You wouldn't be able to keep up the quiet mysterious act if you had a girlfriend."

He stared at me, not saying anything.

"So, instead of having to deal, you stay unattached."

"Until you."

A smile tugged at the corners of my lips. "Until me."

"Why do you think that is?" he asked, surprising me by keeping the conversation going.

"I think we're more alike than you initially thought. I think there's comfort in that for you."

He considered the notion for a moment. "Maybe."

"I also think you found someone incredible, and you knew it would be a monumental mistake if you kept pushing her away. You couldn't let her slip through your fingertips," I teased.

He laughed. "And the princess is back."

I adjusted the nonexistent tiara on my head. "She's never very far."

"I'm glad I let you in, Kresley," he said, the sincerity in his eyes nearly leveling me.

"Me too."

CHAPTER THIRTY
Kresley

For obvious reasons, I did not return to the shelter on Sunday. I met Elodie and Alice for dinner that night. I didn't get to tell them about my date since Tristan and Briggs were both standing nearby, so we texted each other in a group chat from right across the table.

Elodie: What'd u do?

Me: Went on a boat.

They giggled when they read that and Alice typed. **Where?**

Me: A private island.

They squealed causing people around us to turn our way.

I closed my eyes and shook my head, making sure *not* to look in Tristan's direction although I'm sure he could figure out we were talking about him.

Alice: Did you…

I glanced up at them. Their brows bounced in question. I stifled a smile and nodded.

They squealed again.

"Okay, I'm done playing this game," I said aloud.

"But it was so much fun," Alice complained.

I rolled my eyes. "Why don't you two find your own boyfriends? There are plenty of guys out there who could handle the two of you."

"Haven't found them yet," Elodie said.

"Any chance Briggs is single?" Alice asked.

I peeked over my shoulder at him standing against the wall. "I'm not sure. But I can find out."

"We could double date," Alice said.

"Oh, no. Keep me out of it. I have enough issues trying to go on a date with one person."

They laughed.

***

Briggs waited for me in the hallway as I left class on Monday. I looked around, wondering where Tristan was.

"Don't worry. Loverboy's right outside," Briggs said as he continued to focus on the area around us.

"That's not who I was looking for," I lied.

"*Riiiight.*"

"Fine. But if you must know, I refer to him as Dreamboat. Not Loverboy."

He laughed.

"Hey, Briggs. Do you have a girlfriend?"

"Not many women can handle all this man," he said.

I laughed as we stepped outside. He and Alice would definitely make a good pair. Maybe another bowling night was in order.

Students rushed by me in all directions, but still, my eyes found Tristan standing in front of the building, ready to accompany us to my next class.

Tristan stepped in front of us, leading the way as Briggs and I followed him across the quad. The added security gave me peace of mind, especially after what Marco had told me.

My phone rang as we walked. I slipped it out of my back pocket and checked the screen. *Unknown Caller.* I contemplated sending it to voicemail but answered it anyway. "Hello?"

"*Le fou de fortune,*" a familiar French voice purred.

I froze, stopping in place. The hair on the back of my neck stood on end as I looked all around me, certain I'd find him standing in the shadows of the trees.

Tristan and Briggs stopped and looked to me, unsure why I'd stopped.

I pointed desperately to my phone, mouthing to Tristan, "It's him!" I put my phone on speaker so he could hear, but the noise of the busy quad made it difficult.

"Don't bother tracing the call. I won't be on the line long enough," the Frenchman assured me.

"What do you want from me?"

He tsked like he had in my apartment in France, sending a cold chill racing up my spine. "Silly girl. I'm still coming for you."

The crowded quad suddenly began to feel as though it was moving in on me. He could be anywhere. I looked frantically to Tristan who moved his hand, urging me to keep talking as he and Briggs searched the faces around us. "New York is a big place. How will you find me?"

"New York?" he laughed. "I think we both know you were never actually in New York, *le fou de fortune.*"

I swallowed around the lump in my throat. It *had* been his man in the woods. He knew where to find me. Calling me was him showing me that. "Why are you telling me this? Won't it just make me more prepared for you? I can add more security. Install more cameras and alarms."

"Oh, a challenge," he said with false laughter in his voice. "I do love a challenge, especially from such a feisty knife-wielding girl like you."

"I wish it didn't have to come to that," I said, trying to keep him talking. "But you left me no choice."

"It was just an eye," he said.

An eye?

"And though I lost sight in that eye, I've never stopped having my sights set on you. Blinding me just made the reward that much sweeter. *Jusqu'à ce que nous nous revoyions.*"

Until we meet again.

The line went dead. I stood frozen, afraid if I moved, he'd see me.

"He could be here," Briggs whispered as he and Tristan crowded around me.

Tristan called his team at the office, making sure they got whatever they could from the call. Then, he looked to Briggs, avoiding my eyes. "We need to get her back."

They flanked me on both sides, a good thing because sudden lightheadedness swept over me. We began to walk and they kept their eyes on everyone and everything around us as we made our way through the busy quad and down the path to my dorm.

I didn't exhale until I was safely back in my room with Briggs outside my door and Tristan leaned against my desk.

"I just need to think," he said as he dragged his fingers through his hair. "*Fuuuuuck.*"

"Tristan, stop. You're scaring me."

"How hadn't we realized?" he said.

"Realized what?"

"You blinded him."

"I just started stabbing at him." I swallowed hard, the recollection clouding my vision with tears. "I knew he grabbed at his face, but everything happened so fast and then he was gone."

"He wants revenge." Tristan scrubbed his hands up and down his face. "*God, dammit.*"

"*Tristan,*" I pled, needing him to be the calm one.

"When we thought this was just a ransom situation, we could track money exchange. We could follow leads. We could monitor things happening out of France."

"So?"

"This isn't a ransom situation. This is personal."

I searched his face. "Which means what?"

He stared back at me long and hard, so many thoughts playing across his face. "I don't know."

I closed my eyes, my limbs beginning to tremble. Tristan always knew what to do.

"I'm sorry." He rushed to sit down next to me on my bed and wrapped his arm around me, pulling me into his side. "I'm not trying to scare you, it just hit me all at once."

"You're worried about me. I understand that. I'm worried too. He could be here. He could be anywhere trying to get to me."

"I won't let that happen," Tristan promised.

I needed to talk to my parents. I needed to tell them what happened. Why these men had come after me. Why they were *still* coming after me. I needed to go home. I'd be safer at home. This was the first time since coming to Remington that I truly believed that. I needed to think of my parents. They couldn't lose a daughter because I was trying to prove that I was strong. They deserved better than that.

"I think you should go home," Tristan said.

"Me too."

He pulled back and met my gaze. "Yeah?"

I nodded. "This isn't a game. He's really coming for me."

"You'll need to stay home until he's caught," Tristan said with undeniable certainty. "And, that'll take time."

"We could always buy that island," I said, trying to ease the tension in the room.

"I wish I could buy it for you. I wish I could make sure nothing bad ever happens to you again. But I can't. That's obvious now."

I sat up and faced him, stroking his cheek so he met my gaze. "I love you, Tristan." I didn't care if it was too soon. He needed to know how I felt. "I'm sorry if you don't want to hear that, but you are it for me. I think I knew it the first time you sat outside my door. I just didn't want to admit it. But I'm admitting it now."

"Good."

My brows furrowed. "Good?"

"I don't know how any of this is going to play out, but I do know I love the hell out of you."

I laughed, unsure how it was even possible given the circumstances. "I knew it."

He chuckled before leaning in and pressing his lips to mine. I took it as his assurance. That he'd always protect me...*and* my heart.

CHAPTER THIRTY-ONE
Kresley

By three, I'd packed most of my belongings into cardboard boxes Elodie found for me in the maintenance room in the basement. She and Alice were devastated that I'd be finishing the school year online. We'd become close, *and* I was the most entertainment they'd had in a long time.

I pulled down the lights that wrapped around my room, twisting them into a ball and tucking them into a box. I climbed onto my bed and stood on the now bare mattress. I reached up and pulled off the glow-in-the-dark stars one at a time. These were coming home with me. If I wasn't going to be able to see Tristan for a while, at least I'd have the stars to remind me of him.

He'd been packing the car for me, making me stay in my room. He was driving me home, which made me feel better. I didn't want to say goodbye to him here. I wanted him all to myself and safe at my house.

My phone rang and I jumped, expecting the worst. But it was Elodie's name that appeared on the screen. I released a breath and answered it. "Hi."

"*Le fou de fortune,*" the Frenchman said.

A cold shiver surged through me. "Where's Elodie?"

"Is that your friend with the glasses?"

My heart thrashed inside my chest. "Where is she?"

"Talk to her," his voice ordered cruelly.

"I'm so sorry, Kresley," she whimpered, the sound ripping my heart in two.

"Where are you?" I asked, desperate to help her.

"That's enough," the Frenchman snapped, cutting off our conversation.

"Don't hurt her. She has nothing to do with this," I pled.

"Oh. I'm so glad you're seeing things my way, *le fou de fortune.*"

"What do you want?"

"Well, you of course," he said.

"Where are you?"

"Oh, so eager," he purred. "I'm right here. So close to seeing you once again."

"Where?" I practically screamed, losing any calm that remained inside me.

"The basement. Come alone, or I won't hesitate for even a second to end her life."

My stomach dropped along with the floor beneath my feet. "How can I come alone? I have security who won't let me out of their sight."

"Oh, you're creative. You'll figure something out…"

Elodie cried out as he disconnected the call.

Shit, shit, shit!

I knew it was stupid to go down there alone. I knew with every fiber of my being that it was the stupidest idea ever. But my friend's life was on the line. And she had nothing to do with this. Just like Doris at the shelter, I brought danger to her because of my need to live a normal life. My *selfish* need to live a normal life. But I knew now, I was never going to be able to do that. It was just a fairy tale I'd made up in my head. But my life wasn't a fairy tale. It was a nightmare.

And despite every fiber of my being telling me to call for help, *I* needed to stop this.

I needed to do the right thing for Elodie. Not the right thing for me.

I rushed over to my bed with my heart in my throat. I dropped to my knees and reached underneath the mattress, grasping around until I felt the cold metal of the gun Tristan had given me after target practice. I pulled it from the bottom of my mattress and held it in my palm. My hand shook so wildly I almost dropped it.

Would I even be able to pull the trigger?

My knees wobbled as I stood up and tucked the gun into the back of my jeans, making sure my shirt concealed it. I lifted the box that was on my bed, took it to the door, and knocked, letting Briggs know I needed him.

He opened the door. "What's up?"

"Can you please bring this down to Tristan?"

"Why can't you give it to him when he gets back?" he asked.

"Ummm." I swallowed, my nerves wearing thin. "I'm scared and I just want to get out of here."

He cocked his head. "You know I'm not supposed to leave my post."

"Please, Briggs," I said, trying to keep my voice steady as my pulse slammed beneath my skin. "I just really want to be done here."

His eyes narrowed. "Fine. But don't open this door for anyone."

"Thank you, Briggs," I said, both relieved and terrified. He took the box from my hands and waited for me to close the door before heading downstairs.

Once I was alone, I dragged in a deep breath, waited for thirty seconds, then opened my door. I looked out into the hallway. No one was around, so I ran to the stairwell taking the two flights down to the basement.

Dim lights filled the hallway. The whirring of washing machines and dryers in the laundry room echoed in the distance. There were no rooms down there, just storage closets, the maintenance room, and the kitchen where the girls had baked me cookies.

I tiptoed down the hallway, staying close to the wall. I poked my head into the maintenance room. It was jammed with broken chairs and desks, but there was nowhere for two people to hide, especially if the Frenchman wanted me to find him.

I moved to the laundry room, stepping slowly inside. Some of the dryers ran, the clothes inside spinning around behind the glass doors. The washers on the opposite side shook through the spin cycle, and I twisted around, but no one was in there either. I released a shaky breath.

I moved back to the door, peeking out into the hallway. It was empty. I released a breath before stepping into it and creeping slowly to the next room. The small kitchen.

I stepped inside and my eyes took in the old appliances against the wall and the wooden table in the center of the room.

The door I'd walked through slammed shut, and I jumped.

"*Le fou de fortune.*"

A chill rushed through me as I turned. There he was. The Frenchman, taller than I remembered, wearing all black with a patch over his left eye. There was a gun in his hand, dangling at his side.

I steeled my features, though my heart walloped in my chest. "Where's Elodie?"

"Have pleasantries gone out the window?" he asked. "You Americans need to learn a thing or two about geniality."

"Where's Elodie?" I repeated.

"I gave you my word," he said. "You came, and she's free to go."

I looked around, but Elodie wasn't there. "Then let her go," I said, trying so damn hard to sound confident, though all I wanted was to be as far away from him as possible.

He stepped away from the door and slowly circled me as if I were his prey. "Oh, she's free to go…just as soon as we leave. I've secured a private jet since I know it's what you're used to."

Bile crept up the back of my throat as I turned slowly, not letting him get behind me. I knew what he was capable of. "I can call my parents right now. How much do you want and where do you want it sent?" I reached around for my phone in my back pocket.

"Keep your hands where I can see them," he ordered, lifting his gun and pointing it at me. "I may be partially blind but I'm not stupid."

I held up my hands to show him they were empty.

"We'll call them once we're far away from here." He stopped by the counter and snatched a knife out of the cutlery block. The ping of the metal pierced the silence in the kitchen.

Why did he need a knife? He had a gun.

He walked to a door at the side of the room and yanked it open. Elodie and Alice were on their knees in the closet. Their ankles, wrists, and mouths were taped with thick electrical tape, their eyes wide with fear.

I gasped. He'd taken both of them. I stared at them trying to communicate my regret. This all happened because they were kind enough to befriend me. Some friend I turned out to be. "I'm so sorry," I said to them.

"As a show of good faith, I'll leave this knife for them to get free." The Frenchman placed the knife on the table. "Just not too soon. We need to leave first."

"How do you plan to get me out? I have bodyguards who'll be looking for me."

"Oh, *le fou de fortune*," he chuckled. "You really think I'm alone?"

My stomach clenched. Had his men hurt Tristan and Briggs? Is that why they hadn't found me yet? I needed to do something. And I needed to do it quickly. "I want to say goodbye to my friends."

He rolled his single eye.

"I've done everything you asked," I reminded him.

He waved the gun in their direction. "Do not touch them."

I hurried over to them, moving the gun to the front of my jeans as I did so he couldn't see me. I kneeled in front of them. "Are you okay?"

They bobbed their heads but the fear in their eyes remained.

"I'm so sorry this happened. You two have been the best friends a girl could ever ask for." I tried not to cry because I needed to be able to see without tears blurring my vision. "He's leaving the knife so you can get yourselves out of the tape," I assured them. "I never meant to bring danger to your lives."

"Okay. Let's go," the Frenchman said, grasping the back of my shirt and yanking me to my feet.

I prayed he wouldn't deceive me and hurt my friends. I prayed he stayed true to his word. It was me he wanted. Not them.

The door swung open and my head twisted toward it.

Tristan stood there with his gun aimed directly at the Frenchman.

Relief washed over me, but it was short-lived. The Frenchman wrapped his arm around me roughly, holding me in a chokehold and pulling me against him to use me as a shield. "What are you going to do now?" he taunted Tristan while aiming his gun at him.

I dropped my eyes, wanting to let Tristan know I had my gun.

Bang! Bang!

My eyes shot up as Tristan's body was thrust back against the hallway wall.

"*Tristan!*" I screamed, struggling to rush to him, but the Frenchman tightened his hold on me.

"Oh no you don't," he said.

Blood spread through Tristan's shirt like a rush of ink above his heart and at his hip. Somehow, he kept himself braced against the wall and lifted his gun, aiming it at us with his eyes trained on the Frenchman. But since I was still his shield, Tristan couldn't shoot him.

My body trembled as I watched the color draining from Tristan's face. He needed help and he needed it fast.

"What are you gonna do now, bodyguard?" The Frenchman snickered, the sound cold and mocking. "Do you save her or save yourself?"

The mocking sound of his laughter mixed with my fear of losing Tristan gave me the nerve I needed. I reach for the gun in my jeans. With shaking hands, I released the safety like Tristan had shown me while it was still tucked in my jeans.

The Frenchman was too busy taunting Tristan to notice me slip the gun from my jeans "I had no trouble shooting her other bodyguard either," he continued. "Did he make it or did he end up six feet under?"

I spread my legs and aimed the gun down at his feet. I closed my eyes, hoping to God I hit him and not me, and fired.

Bang!

"What the—" The Frenchman released his grip on me as he jumped back, startled by the unexpected sound and uncertainty of where the bullet hit.

I ducked away from him, and that was all the time Tristan needed. The sound of his gunfire echoed through the small kitchen.

Elodie and Alice screamed beneath their tape.

The Frenchman staggered back, but not before turning his gun on me.

I froze, my eyes wide and my heart in my throat.

Bang!

I recoiled, nearly jumping out of my skin.

But the bullet hadn't hit me.

It hit the Frenchman square in the forehead.

I looked away from the gory sight as his body was thrust into the counter behind him.

I looked to Tristan whose gun was still extended. I rushed over to him. The blood on his shirt had spread, covering most of it. "Oh my God. Please be okay."

"I'm fine," he said, though I knew he wasn't. "Baby, you did so damn good."

My head spun, and I felt lightheadedness wash over me. I pulled in a deep breath and focused, needing to get him help. *I* needed to be the strong one. I pulled out my phone to call for help, but my hand shook so wildly I almost couldn't dial. Once I did, I lifted the phone to my ear. "We're in the basement of Gorham Hall at Remington University. Send police and an ambulance!"

I hung up and looked to Tristan who moved to the Frenchman's body, now strewn on the floor. Though he was clearly dead, Tristan kicked the gun away from him. Not taking any chances.

"Please tell me you're gonna be okay," I said, needing his reassurance.

"They're just flesh wounds," he assured me, before calling Briggs.

I grabbed the knife from the table and rushed over to Elodie and Alice. I pulled the tape from their mouths and they dragged in gulps of air.

"Oh, my God," Elodie said as tears trailed down her cheeks.

"Is it over?" Alice asked through her own tears.

I slit the tape at their ankles and wrists. Then, they both threw their arms around me and held on tightly.

"That was so scary," Elodie said. "I thought he'd kill us."

"I'm so sorry," I said, feeling nothing but regret for bringing danger to them.

"We're gonna be okay," Alice said. "All of us."

Sirens bellowed outside the building.

I released the girls and turned to Tristan who was digging in the Frenchman's pockets.

He stood up, but the color had completely drained from his face.

"You're losing a lot of blood," I said. "You need an ambulance."

"I need to make sure whoever showed up with him is not here anymore."

Someone rushed through the kitchen door and we all instinctively shuffled backward.

It was Briggs.

Sighs of relief rushed out of us.

Briggs' eyes landed on the dead Frenchman. "Nice work."

"Did you find the others?" Tristan asked.

Briggs noticed his wounds. "You all right, man?"

"He needs an ambulance," I said.

"There was just one other guy," Briggs explained, knowing Tristan would not budge until he knew. "The cops have him in custody and his story checks out. Footage from the airport shows the two of them flew in alone."

I released a long breath, terrified to actually allow myself to believe that all of this might really be over.

EMTs entered the room. One rushed over to the Frenchman, while the others checked on Tristan.

Tristan glanced to me. I could tell he was thinking the same thing as me.

"It's over," I said.

CHAPTER THIRTY-TWO
Kresley

"How are you?" Tristan asked, squeezing my hand from the seat beside me in my father's private jet.

"The same as when you asked me ten minutes ago," I said, trying not to snap at him.

"And that is…?"

"Angry that my boyfriend, who just underwent major surgery, insisted on checking himself out of the hospital against doctor's wishes to accompany me home."

"I'm fine," he assured me, though the stitches in his shoulder and hip would argue otherwise.

"But are you?" I pressed. "Because you scared the hell out of me."

"It's all part of the job," he said. "How are you? You scared me when you pulled out that gun."

"It's all part of the job," I said straight-faced, trying my hardest to push the vision of the dead Frenchman from my mind. The dead Frenchman Tristan killed for me. The one who put two bullets in my boyfriend because of me.

"It'd be okay if you weren't okay," Tristan said, shooting me a sad smile.

"I know." I stared out the window watching the clouds blur past the window with so many haphazard thoughts whirling through my brain.

"A penny for your thoughts," Tristan said, clearly knowing I was overwhelmed with everything that had occurred over the past twenty-four hours.

I turned to look at him with something weighing heavy on my mind. "I need to say something."

"Okay," he urged.

"And I don't want to upset you."

"Nothing you say could upset me, unless you're kicking my ass to the curb."

I rolled my eyes, knowing nothing could make me break it off with the guy who saved me so many times—in more ways than one. "I know I'll never get the chance to meet your parents, but I have a few things I really would've liked to tell them."

His eyes narrowed, his brows drawn in question. "Like what?"

"Well…I'd start by telling them that you're the bravest person I know."

He rolled his eyes.

"And, even though you don't like it when I say it, you're like a real-life superhero." I ignored the snarl that left him and continued. "I know you wish more than anything that you could go back to that day when you were nine and change the outcome. But I'd want them to know, you're doing everything in your power to make up for it now. And succeeding. I mean, you've saved me *twice*."

"*Kres*," he pled.

I ignored his plea. "I'd also tell them that they raised an amazing boy who grew into an amazing man. One who's strong and confident and would put his life on the line for the people he swears to protect. Whether he likes them at first or not."

His soft laughter filled the plane.

"Oh, and I'd ask who you got your looks from because you're a total babe."

His smile told me I hadn't pushed him too far by bringing up his parents. And hopefully, he'd see that he hadn't let them down. Hopefully, he'd see that he'd done right by them. It was one thing for me to tell him that. But it was another for him to hear that I wanted to tell *them* that. Now, maybe his sleep would no longer be plagued with nightmares of what he couldn't control. Maybe now he'd sleep. Because he deserved to sleep.

EPILOGUE
One Month Later
Kresley

We'd been swimming all day and now lounged in our bathing suits on a blanket on the deserted beach. I rested my head on Tristan's chest and could hear his steady heartbeat beneath my ear. My finger drifted from the scar on his shoulder to the one on his hip. Some girls needed their boyfriends to get tattoos that represented them or their love for them. Mine was permanently scarred as a reminder of what he'd done for me.

The sun was just setting, and I couldn't wait to take in the stars with no lights obscuring our view. We'd been on the island for the past two days since my parents had been gracious enough to rent it for us. They were eager to do whatever it took to make me feel safe again. Since I had my very own bodyguard who'd taken two bullets and killed two men for me, it provided them the peace of mind they needed. Not to mention, we had bodyguards on boats around the island. So, yeah. There was that too.

"Did you submit your assignment?" Tristan asked.

I nodded. "Now I just need to worry about exams."

"I'm sure you'll ace them," he said.

"Obviously."

A long silence passed as the ocean waves crashed and the briny air worked its way into my senses.

"Can I ask you something?" Tristan said.

"Uh oh. That sounds ominous."

"For someone who loves to talk, why don't you ever talk about what happened?" he asked.

He'd been good about not talking about it—which I appreciated, so I had a feeling I knew why he'd brought it up now. "Did my parents get to you, too?"

"What?"

"They think because I don't talk about it, I must need more counseling. Like I'm bottling it all up."

"Are you?" he asked with worry in his voice.

"Not even a little bit. I feel…at peace." I turned my head and rested my chin on his chest so I could see his eyes. "Absolutely. He was a bad man who wanted to hurt me and the people I care about. How could I regret what happened? I know he's not out there anymore. He doesn't even inhabit my dreams. I sleep now."

"I thought that was because I'm next to you?"

I smiled. "That too."

He tightened his arms around me, and I knew how proud of me he was. He didn't have to say it. I could see it in everything he did and every look he gave me. "I'm never gonna live it down that you were the one to distract him," Tristan said.

"It was time that someone saved you, Tristan Stone. Now we're almost even."

He shook his head. "You saved me long before that, Kres. I was floundering in darkness, trying to conquer my nightmares—my regrets—by protecting other people. And you were just this light that came rushing in. I fought it the best I could, but you won out. You deserve the cape, Kres. Not the other way around."

I pressed a kiss to his chest, not needing to respond to such a sweet sentiment.

Darkness soon crept over our island and the stars began to speckle the early night sky.

"Marco needs me back to work next week," Tristan said. "He thinks the longer I'm off on an island with you, the more I won't want to come back."

"He's a father to a daughter now. His life is irrevocably changed. He's gonna grow into this big softy so he needs his tough partner back," I said.

Taking me by surprise, Tristan rolled over, covering me with his body and resting on top of me so he could look me in the eyes. "But what do *you* need?"

I thought for a moment. "I just need you."

His brows shot up. "Forever?"

I nodded.

"Good." He reached into our beach bag and dug around. When he pulled his hand back out, he held a diamond ring.

My eyes widened.

"Nothing about us has been normal. Like, the complete *opposite* of normal," he began.

I laughed.

"But I can't imagine going through this life with anyone other than you, Kres. You're strong, you're brave, you're funny, you're high maintenance—"

"*Hey.*"

He smiled. "I was kidding about that one. But I'm not kidding when I say that I love everything about you and want to keep you safe for the rest of our lives. Marry me."

I could've burst with the amount of happiness rushing through me. He'd been right. Nothing about us had been normal, but there was no denying we'd been meant for each other. We had so much in common. The similar things we'd been through, our shared experiences, and our ability to push each other's buttons like no other. But it all added up to one thing. There was no one out there in this world who could handle us. So, I did the only thing I could when expectant Caribbean blue eyes stared back at me. I nodded my head.

"Yes?"

"Yes, yes, *yeeeeees!*"

He leaned down and pressed his lips to mine, kissing me with so much love I could feel it coursing through my body.

I pulled out of the kiss with a smile on my face. "But you're only twenty-five. You sure you should be getting married?"

He smirked recalling our conversation in my dorm room. "People get married at all ages."

"If they're crazy," I said, using his words on him.

"Oh, we're definitely crazy."

"May I have my ring now?" I asked, holding out my hand and wiggling my fingers anxiously.

He slipped the ring onto my finger. It was gorgeous just like his proposal. "Thank you, Tristan," I said, sincerity replacing my humor. "I'm going to make you the happiest man in this entire world."

He shook his head. "Not possible."

My brows pinched together.

"I already am."

THE END

MORE FROM J. NATHAN

For You Standalone Sports Series:
Book #1 *For Finlay*
Book #2 *For Forester*
Book #3 *For Crosby*
Book #4 *For Emery*

Savage Beasts Standalone Rock Star Series:
Book #1 *Kozart*
Book #2 *Treyton*

Standalones:
Seren
Something About You
You're the Reason
Until Alex
Before Hadley
Since Drew

ACKNOWLEDGEMENTS

Thank you so much for taking the time to read Kresley and Tristan's story. I hope you enjoyed it as much as I enjoyed writing it!

To all the bloggers and readers who share my books. I could never do this without all of you! Thank you so much!

To my wonderful ARC team members who read and review my books. I am so lucky to have such a great team behind me!

To my reader's group, *J. Nathan's Book Boyfriend Lovers.* Thank you for being a fun place for me to go to post about my books and life. Your friendship means the world to me!

To my wonderful beta readers: Dali, Renee, Kim, Megan, Maria, and Heather. Thank you for your feedback. I know this book was a little different for me, so I appreciated your honest critiques! You definitely made the story stronger.

To my editor Stephanie Elliot. Thank you for being so tough on me. This book required so much of your time and for that I am forever thankful!

To my wonderful proofreaders, Gem from Gem's Precise Proofreading and Peggy. I don't know what I'd do without the two of you catching my last-minute mistakes. Thank you so much!! You're both amazing!! And, yes, Gemma. Tristan can be yours!

To my amazing PA Renee. This book would not have made it out to the world without you telling me it was good enough, even when I wasn't sure!!

To Kate Farlow at Y'all. That Graphic for creating another beautiful cover and teasers. Thank you for your patience and assistance—even in the middle of a hurricane with no power!!

To photographer Brian Kaminski for the gorgeous photo of the wonderful Jake Hobbs. Thank you for making it happen! You were incredible to work with—even sending me photos while you were out of town! I hope we can work together again very soon!!

A big thank you to Grey's PR for all of your assistance. You are all so lovely to work with.

To Inga at Magic Pen Book Tours for reaching out to help spread the word for me. You are a true professional, and I see great things for your company!

To my family. Thank you for always supporting me. I am one lucky girl!

ABOUT THE AUTHOR

J. Nathan resides on the east coast with her husband and ten-year-old son. She is an avid reader of all things romance. Happy endings are a must. Alpha males with chips on their shoulders are an added bonus. When she's not curled up with a good book, she can be found spending time with family and friends, at soccer and baseball games cheering on her son, and working on her next novel.